That was th ...
Abigail conce ...

Nick Harrington was like an intricate puzzle that you could spend the rest of your life trying to get to the bottom of.

The sensual mouth had curved into a slow, humourless smile. 'You've grown up, Abby,' he observed, with a touch of wry surprise. 'That was a pretty thorough inspection you just subjected me to.'

'And does it bother you?' she queried coolly.

'A beautiful girl giving me the once-over?' he mocked. 'Who in their right mind would object to that? Though to be scrupulously fair, Abby, I really ought to return the compliment…'

Sharon Kendrick was born in West London and has had *heaps* of jobs which include photography, nursing, driving an ambulance across the Australian desert and cooking her way around Europe in a converted double-decker bus! Without a doubt, writing is the best job she has ever had, and when she's not dreaming up new heroes (some of which are based on her doctor husband!), she likes cooking, reading, theatre, listening to American west coast music and talking to her two children, Celia and Patrick.

Recent titles by the same author:

THAT KIND
OF MAN

BY
SHARON KENDRICK

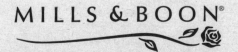

MILLS & BOON®

To Rosie and Adam for still trying to set the world to rights!

First published in Great Britain 1997
Harlequin Mills & Boon Limited,
Eton House, 18-24 Paradise Road, Richmond, Surrey TW9 1SR

© Sharon Kendrick 1997

ISBN 0 263 80535 2

Set in Times Roman 11 on 12 pt.
01-9801-43388 C1

Printed and bound in Great Britain
by Mackays of Chatham PLC, Chatham

CHAPTER ONE

'OH, ORLANDO! Darling, darling Orlando!' An unknown blonde wearing black gave a dramatic cry.

Abigail had noticed the woman in church. She had been sobbing loudly throughout the service, but now Abigail could observe that the tears she had cried had left her mascara miraculously unsmudged. She had wondered briefly whether the woman had been one of her husband's lovers, before pulling herself up short—for that way lay madness.

The bitter wind lifted a stray strand of honey-coloured hair and whipped it across Abigail's pale face, and the gentle lashing movement forced her to give herself a little shake. Because it was all like a dream—some weird and crazy dream. Not a nightmare exactly, but something pretty close to it. Unreal. Yes, that was it. Unreal. As if this were all happening to someone else. And not to her.

Abigail shivered violently as a fat flake of snow fluttered down from the gun-metal sky like a frenzied bird, to eventually settle on her hand. She had worn a pair of fine black kid gloves in an attempt to keep warm, but, even so, her fingers still shook like a drunk's as they clutched onto a single scarlet rose.

She was cold. Cold as an arctic waste. Unprotected from the furies of the winter weather, she stood by the graveside wearing the only black outfit she had had in her wardrobe—a thin, two-piece suit whose material, if not colour, was more suited to a spring day.

Black was not a colour she normally wore, but for today it was a must. And Orlando would have expected it. Because no matter what had gone on between them—no matter what a mess their marriage had been—he should not have died.

She was too young, she thought, casting a disbelieving look around her. Much too young to be a widow at nineteen, standing with and yet curiously apart from Orlando's wild, thespian friends, who even now were loudly reciting extravagant poetry. How she wished that they would stop. During their histrionics at the church she had been half tempted to tell them to shut up, but the last thing she wanted today, of all days, was a row.

If only she had someone there for her. Someone to rely on. Someone strong enough to lean on. Or at least to cast a few withering looks of disapproval which might make some of the people present behave more circumspectly.

But she had no one. Her mother was dead, her beloved stepfather was dead—both killed in a horrific car crash just months before her wedding. It seemed that everyone she loved was taken away from her. The only person she had left in the world was Nick, and theirs was only the most tenuous link—a link that was always in danger of being broken by their mutual dislike.

Because Nick Harrington had resented her since the moment he had first set eyes on her, on what should have been one of the happiest days of her life...

She had been sitting on her stepfather's shoulders at the time. Philip Chenery had been proudly carrying her into the vast hallway of his mansion, tucked away high up in the Hollywood Hills.

Abigail had been breathless with excitement. The day before, her beautiful actress mother had become Mrs Philip Chenery in the most fairytale wedding ceremony Abigail could have imagined. Her mother had married one of Hollywood's biggest producers, and the three of them were going to live happily ever after in the most glamorous house in the world.

In the shiny marbled hallway, all the staff had lined up to meet Philip's new wife and her young daughter—and Nick, as the son of Philip's cook, had been scowlingly forced to stand in line too.

Abigail had only been seven at the time. Some psychologists said that it was impossible to remember that far back. But Abigail did. The memory of meeting Nick Harrington was scorched onto her mind for ever and a day.

She would never forget the way those clever, slanting green eyes had fixed her coolly in their sights. The eighteen-year-old boy had already possessed a heart-breakingly handsome face, but it was a proud and cold face. He hadn't shown a flicker of emotion as he'd stared at her, but Abigail had immediately sensed his disapproval.

The product of a ravishing Italian mother and a

brilliant English father, Nick Harrington had inherited all the very best characteristics from both nationalities. His keen, natural intelligence and outrageously good looks ensured that men would always try to emulate him and women would spend a lifetime casting hungry glances in his direction.

Abigail had discovered later that Philip had a soft spot for the boy, whose father had abandoned him just as her own father had abandoned her. He had recognised Nick's outstanding potential immediately and had invested in his education. Not surprisingly, the two of them had formed a close bond.

So perhaps it was only natural that Nick should have resented Abigail. She was, after all, trespassing on his territory.

Abigail had seen it differently.

She'd been a small girl already thrust into a brand-new life, miles away from England, and Nick's attitude had unsettled her. Nick Harrington had been the serpent in her paradise, and, because of it, a silent bond of enmity had been born.

She had been grateful that he was more than a decade her senior, that she had been sent far away to her mother's old boarding-school in England, and that their meetings were destined to be brief, during her school vacations.

As she had grown older she had supposed that the animosity might die a natural death, but her supposition had been wrong. Nick had seemed to resent her more as each year passed, and when she had blossomed into womanhood it had got even worse—he had actually seemed to despise her. So she just did the sensible thing and despised him right back.

Yes, there was certainly no love lost between her and Nick Harrington.

And yet...

It was stupid, really, but at times today she had found herself wishing that he had bothered to come to her husband's funeral. Nick's might not be a face she welcomed seeing in normal circumstances, but at least it was a familiar face. And right now she longed for the sight of something familiar, for she was as lonely as she could ever remember feeling.

But, in response to the news of Orlando's death, there had been nothing more than an exquisite display of pure white lilies and a brief, almost curt letter of condolence which had given Abigail little comfort.

No phone call. No appearance at the church—even though she had craned her neck to look for his dark head rising above all the others...

The priest was now intoning the final words of farewell as the coffin was slowly lowered into the earth and Abigail raised the hand which still clutched the rose so tightly.

A chill breeze briefly lifted the delicate scarlet petals of the rose upwards, so that they flapped like wings, and then Abigail threw it down onto the coffin, with the kind of dramatic gesture she knew her late husband would have appreciated.

Then, without knowing why she did it, she tore the black kid gloves from her pale hands and hurled them away from her, so that they, too, slowly fluttered down to alight on top of the polished coffin.

She raised her pale, strained face, a sudden movement catching her attention, and she felt an odd, prickling sensation as she looked up and found herself staring directly into Nick Harrington's enigmatic eyes—as cold and as green as a northern fiord.

He stood apart from the rest of the mourners, tall and lean, his dark, handsome face cruel and arrogant and proud. The narrow-eyed look he threw at Abigail was one of pure challenge.

She felt as though she had been woken from a long and drugged sleep—her senses leaping into life as though they had been newly born. Just the shock of seeing him again made Abigail's heart contract painfully in her chest. She felt all the blood drain from her cheeks and, just for a second, she had to fight to stay upright.

He gave her a brief, frowning scrutiny as he observed her reaction, and then began walking rapidly towards her until he was standing in front of her, towering over her like some dark, malevolent statue.

And Abigail found herself having to strain her neck to stare upwards at him, even though she was wearing high, rather tottery black heels. Each time she saw him she was always slightly amazed by his impressive height and extraordinary presence—as though her memory was somehow defective where Nick Harrington was concerned.

'Hello, Abigail,' he said quietly, in that deep, slumberous voice whose accent defied description. But that was hardly surprising—he had been educated at the finest universities in the world. He was the original nomad—a rich, successful nomad, with his fancy homes and his rare paintings and fast cars.

She had not seen him since the eve of her wedding, close on a year ago, when he had been so unbearably rude to Orlando. And to her. When he had arrived at their hotel as if he owned the place, had coldly summoned them into his presence and threatened to call a halt to the wedding.

But he hadn't been able to.

And how wonderful it had been to see the powerful Nick Harrington impotent for once! Unable to exert his formidable will to shape the future. Like a precious gift, Abigail had treasured the memory of his dark, implacable face as she had made her wedding vows in Chelsea's famous Register Office.

Come to think of it, his face looked just as forbidding and implacable right now. 'Hello, Nick,' she responded calmly.

'How are you, Abby?' he said softly, and the concern in his voice sounded almost genuine.

'I'm, I'm…,' she responded falteringly, only it all came out in a kind of wobbly gulp. Perhaps it was the concern that did it, or the use of her childhood nickname, or maybe even the unaccustomed gentleness in his voice. Because for the first time since Orlando's death Abigail felt the salt taste of tears welling up at the back of her throat. She made a small, choking sound, terrified that she was going to break down in front of him.

He frowned again deeply, as if any show of vulnerability was distasteful to him. 'Are you okay?' He gave her a narrow-eyed look of interrogation and seemed half inclined to take her elbow, but then appeared to think better of it. He pushed his hands deep into the pockets of his grey trousers, and Abigail was appalled to find herself noticing how the fine fabric stretched almost indecently over his muscular thighs. 'Are you okay?' he repeated.

'What do you think?' she asked bitterly, because he was the only person in the world she could take it out on right now. Because surely Nick, more than anyone, knew how unfair life could be?

'I don't think you'd care to hear what I think,' he said, in a bitter, impatient kind of voice, and Abigail's head jerked up in surprise at the underlying menace she heard there.

He might not be her favourite person in the world, but at this precise moment he was her only lifeline, the person closest to her, who knew her better than anyone else in the world. Could bridges not be mended in troubled times? 'I would,' she answered quietly, her heavy-lidded blue eyes bright with unshed tears and filled with appeal as she sought for clever, confident Nick to make some sense of it all. 'Tell me what you think about it, Nick?' she appealed.

But he merely shook his dark head. 'I'm sorry,' he said, in a bland, steady voice, 'about Orlando.'

Some small, vague hope which had flared up inside Abigail was snuffed out. She had never thought that Nick would be the kind of person simply to spout out polite platitudes. She lifted her chin squarely and looked him full in the eye. 'I could have accused you of many things, Nick Harrington,' she told him proudly, 'but never of hypocrisy! How have you got the nerve to stand there and say you're *sorry*, when everyone knows what you really thought of Orlando?'

He didn't flinch, his unwavering green gaze not tainted by an iota of guilt. 'Just because I didn't like him—'

'Hated him, you mean,' she corrected fiercely.

He shook his head. 'Everything's always so black and white for you, isn't it, Abigail?' He sighed, as if it gave him little pleasure to say the words. 'Hate is too strong an emotion to use in connection with Orlando. You have to feel passion before you can hate someone, and I couldn't summon up enough energy to feel hatred for a man I did not respect.'

'No, of course you couldn't!' agreed Abigail caustically. 'Any emotion other than the desire to make money is too strong for Mr cold-fish-Harrington, isn't it?'

He gave her a long, steady look. 'At the moment, the overwhelming emotion I'm experiencing is a desire to put you over my knee,' he said evenly, 'and beat some of that damned cynicism out of you!'

His eyes narrowed and he seemed to be measuring his words carefully. 'Just because I didn't like the man, it doesn't mean I wanted to see him dead, Abigail. To die at any age is a tragedy, but to die when you're only twenty-five is a waste. An utter,

utter waste.' His mouth thinned into a disapproving line. 'What happened? Was he drunk when he died?'

'He was *abseiling*, for heaven's sake!' she responded in an outraged tone. 'He would hardly be drunk!'

Broad shoulders were shrugged dismissively, but the expression in those grass-green eyes was sombre. 'Rumour has it that Orlando was a man in search of cheap thrills. Any kind of thrills. So maybe marriage didn't quite match up to his expectations, hmm, Abby?'

The implication behind his words was shocking. Automatically, and oblivious to the now silent stares of the other mourners, Abigail's hand flailed up to slap him. But his reflexes were lightning-fast, and he caught it just as it was about to connect with his cheek and held it there, so that to an outside observer it looked almost as though she was about to stroke his face and he was letting her. No. Not just letting her. Encouraging her.

Her fingers inadvertently brushed against his cheek, and his skin felt like warm satin. Incredibly, she found herself wanting to stay like that. Just like that.

Angrily, a guilty blush staining her face with its stinging heat, Abigail snatched her hand away, but not before she had surprised a cold little glint of triumph lurking in the depths of his green eyes. In some mad, shaming way, she felt as though she had been compromised.

'Don't you ever dare do anything like that again,' she said in a fierce undertone, and then heard a gentle

cough behind her. She spun round to find the elderly
priest standing there, looking almost apologetic, and
Abigail guiltily realised that the service had come to
an end.

And she hadn't even noticed; she had been far too
busy sparring with Nick. What must the priest think
of her?

'If you feel the need to talk any time, Mrs Howard,'
the priest was saying, in the soothing kind of voice
he had used on innumerable occasions before, 'any
time at all, then please do. My door is always open
for you, my dear. You know that.'

His genuine kindness affected her as much as anything had done that day, and Abigail felt her throat
uselessly constricting as she struggled to find words
to respond to him. Did Nick notice her discomfort?
Was that why he chose to answer when she could not?

'Thank you, Father,' he said smoothly. 'I know that
Abigail will bear that in mind. But I'm here now.'

'Indeed?' The priest looked up at him almost absently from behind the tiny, half-moon-shaped spectacles he wore. 'And you are…? I'm sorry, but I don't
think we've met.'

'I'm Nick Harrington,' came the decisive response,
and then, because the priest seemed to be waiting for
some further explanation, he added, 'An old friend of
the family. I have known Abigail since she was a little
girl. Her late stepfather was a great friend to me.'

'I see.' The priest nodded. 'Well, I'm very pleased
to meet you, Mr Harrington.'

He was probably relieved, thought Abigail, watch-

ing as the two men shook hands. He had been up to
the house several times since Orlando's death, saying
that she really ought to have someone with her.

She remembered him standing in his shabby cas-
sock, looking around the sumptuous drawing-room
with a curious and yet bewildered expression. As
though confused by the fact that Abigail had all the
material possessions anyone could ever possibly want,
and yet she had no one to come and sit with her and
hold her hand while she mourned her dead husband.

'It's time we were leaving,' said Nick in a low
voice. Only this time he did take Abigail's elbow,
holding onto it firmly, as if he was afraid that she
might stumble and fall. And Abigail let him guide her,
grateful for the support he offered.

'Won't you come back to the house for some lunch,
Father?' he was saying to the priest. 'Some of the
others have already set off, I see.' His disapproving
gaze took in Orlando's friends, who were noisily
wending their way towards the long line of black lim-
ousines as though it were a wedding and not a funeral.

One of the women, a dark, elfin creature named
Jemima, was tossing a black feather boa flamboyantly
across one slim, couture-clad shoulder, her glossy
black head flung back in a gesture of extravagant
laughter.

Abigail noticed the twist of scorn which had hardened Nick's mouth into a forbidding line, and wondered what he and the priest must be thinking of this
whole bizarre funeral.

But the priest, at least, seemed oblivious to Nick's

disapproval, and nodded his bald head with enthusiasm. 'Lunch would be very welcome,' he said eagerly, 'and I'd be delighted to join you. Friday happens to be my housekeeper's day off and she usually leaves me a fish salad which, frankly, leaves rather a lot to be desired! I'll walk up to the house—it isn't very far.'

'No, no. It's much too far.' Nick shook his dark head. 'Please take my car,' he said, and pointed to the longest of the low black vehicles which stood in line. 'Really, I insist.'

'But what about you?' asked the priest.

'I'll go with Mrs Howard,' answered Nick, and his eyes defied Abigail to argue with him.

But she was past caring, or arguing. She was numb and cold and exhausted. She let Nick propel her towards one of the waiting cars as though she were a mannequin in a shop-window—her limbs light and useless as if they had been fashioned from plastic. The lethargy which had been plaguing her for days began insidiously to overwhelm her.

She sank down on the squashy black leather seat and closed her eyes, expecting a barrage of questions, but when none came she opened them again and found him observing her, his face curiously expressionless. And that in itself was surprising. Normally there was at least dislike or disapproval on the face of Nick Harrington when he was in her company.

Outside the car, the trees were like charcoal line-drawings etched in stark contrast against heavy grey snow-clouds, and oddly childlike. It was funny, she thought suddenly, but even in the early days of their relationship, when they had been relatively happy, she and Orlando had never discussed having children. Abigail shivered. Not funny at all, really.

Nick saw the shiver and rapped on the glass immediately. 'Could you increase the heating?' he instructed the driver curtly. 'It's like Siberia in the back here.'

A welcome, warm blast of air hit Abigail immediately and she expelled a breath of relief as some of the icy chill left her body.

She seemed to have been cold for days now, a dull, bone-deep coldness she couldn't shift, not since the night the policeman had knocked on the heavy oak door and had waited to give her the momentous news.

She had known immediately that her husband was dead, from the grim look on the policeman's face, but long, agonising seconds had passed before he had asked her that chillingly final question, 'Are you the wife of a Mr Orlando Howard?'

There had been shock at first, deep and profound shock, but hot on its heels had come relief. Blessed relief that Orlando could never taunt her again.

And Abigail had had to live with the guilt of those feelings ever since...

'Are you okay?' Nick's deep voice seemed to come from out of nowhere, and Abigail forced herself back to the present with an effort.

'I suppose so.' She nodded her head stiffly. That dream-like feeling had washed over her again, and all her reflexes seemed to be on auto-pilot. It seemed easier to cope when she felt that way.

'You'll feel better now that the funeral is over.' His eyes were fixed on her face, like a doctor waiting for a reaction from a patient.

'Yes,' she replied. But will I, she wondered? Would she ever feel better again?

'You look tired, Abby,' he observed neutrally. 'Exhausted, in fact.'

'I am.'

'Then rest,' he urged. 'At least until we get back to the house.'

Her normal response to him—if any of her responses to Nick could ever be described as normal—would have been to tell him to mind his own business. His high-handedness was something she usually resented. But he was right, she *was* too exhausted—even to resist him.

Abigail tried to lean her head back, but the hat she wore prevented her from doing so. She lifted her hand and removed first the pin securing it and then the black, wide-brimmed, rather exotic creation from her head.

She never wore hats as a rule, she found them too constricting. She had chosen this one today because Orlando had loved hats, the more outrageous the better. And she had failed him in so many ways as a wife. The least she could do was to don a fancy hat in his honour—to play the part he would have wanted her to play at his funeral.

But it was such a relief to remove it. She tossed it

on the seat beside her and shook her head vigorously, allowing the thick, straight honey-coloured hair to fall down unfettered around her shoulders.

Nick was watching her, his eyes narrowed as the bright hair spilled down in contrast against the black suit, and it was several moments before he spoke. 'You didn't contact me directly when Orlando was killed.'

It was as much a question as a statement, Abigail acknowledged. Almost an accusation, too. She absently pushed a lock of hair off her pale cheek. 'I didn't see the point. I knew that you'd read about it in the papers. We haven't exactly been living in each other's pockets since my marriage, have we? Or before it either, come to that. And you never bothered to hide your dislike of Orlando.'

'The feeling was entirely mutual. Orlando made no secret of his aversion to me, you know.'

Stung into defence, Abigail sat up in her seat. 'He, at least, had a *reason* for disliking you!'

'Oh?' The green gaze was unperturbed. 'And what was that? Envy of my material status? Because if there was ever a man who demonstrated avarice like it was going out of fashion, then it was Orlando.'

'Why, you…you…unbearable brute!' Abigail only got the words out with a monumental effort. 'How can you speak so ill of the dead!'

'I said the same when he was alive, and to his face,' Nick contradicted coolly. 'The reason Orlando hated me was because he was a failure and I wasn't. And because he knew that if I'd stuck around I might just have been able to knock some sense into your pretty but dense little head and stopped you marrying him.'

Disbelief stirred in the depths of Abigail's eyes, so dark blue that they looked like ink. 'You really think you would have been able to stop me marrying him?'

He shrugged. 'It was a pity that he managed to talk you into a register office wedding which could be performed relatively quickly.'

'That made a difference, did it?' she challenged.

His eyes glittered. 'Of course it made a difference. You see, I had rather counted on your love of the big occasion coming to the fore, Abigail. You aren't your mother's daughter for nothing. And if you had opted for a church wedding and all that it entailed, then it would have given me plenty of time to have changed your mind.'

Abigail gave a bitter laugh. 'And you bother asking why I didn't contact you after Orlando died? I can only wonder why you turned up today at all.'

'Because I'm the closest thing to a relative you have,' he pointed out coolly.

'I know,' Abigail's voice was heavy with sarcasm. 'And aren't I the lucky one?'

'Aren't you just?' he agreed mockingly, and stretched his long legs out in front of him.

She had been trying very hard not to look at him too closely, and she didn't want to ask herself why. But that unconsciously graceful stretch made her acutely aware of his physical presence and she found herself unable to tear her eyes away from him.

Even among very good-looking men Nick had always stood out from the crowd. Over the years Abigail had tried to analyse his particular appeal, and once again she attempted to be objective as she watched him covertly from beneath the thick, dark sweep of her eyelashes.

No one could deny that he had a superb physique. He was lightly tanned and muscular, without an ounce of spare flesh lurking on that impressive frame.

But loads of men had good bodies, she reasoned. Orlando, her late husband, had possessed a magnificent physique, which he had shown off whenever possible by wearing the most clinging and revealing clothes he could get away with.

And that, supposed Abigail, was the difference. Nick didn't emphasise his shape; he didn't have to. It would have been glaringly obvious to even the most unobservant person that Nick had a body to die for—even if he'd been swathed in sackcloth. The loose-cut suit he wore now, for example, merely hinted at the flat, hard planes of his abdomen and the heavily muscled thighs which lay beneath, and Abigail felt an uncomfortable awareness of his proximity tickling away at her nerve-ends.

But it was his face which had always drawn women to Nick, and it wasn't just the pure, clean lines of his classically even features which attracted them. Or the curiously sensual curve of his mouth, its softness so at odds with the hard, jutting jaw which lay beneath. No, it was something beyond mere beauty which had held so many women in thrall.

His eyes were as alive and as green as grass, framed

by lashes so thick and black and lush that just looking at them felt sinful.

But it was more than that. His eyes were watchful and wary, too. At times they seemed almost calculating—although calculating what, it was impossible to say. His eyes held secrets.

And that was the main attraction, Abigail conceded reluctantly. Nick Harrington was like an intricate puzzle that you could spend the rest of your life trying to get to the bottom of.

The sensual mouth had curved into a slow, humourless smile. 'You've grown up, Abby,' he observed, with a touch of wry surprise. 'That was a pretty thorough inspection you just subjected me to.'

Her mouth thinned slightly as she met his curious green gaze. Grown up? How right he was. Marriage to Orlando had made her grow up in a big way. 'And does it bother you?' she queried coolly.

'A beautiful girl giving me the once-over?' he mocked. 'Who in their right mind would object to that? Though to be scrupulously fair, Abby, I really ought to return the compliment. Oughtn't I?'

For a moment she was confused, and then, with a rapidly thudding heart, she saw exactly what he meant.

He let his gaze linger from breast to hip, on the long line of her legs which were outlined by the thin material of her black skirt. His eyes roved over her with such a careless, almost insolent appraisal that Abigail found herself blushing furiously, and fastened her hands tightly onto the lapels of her jacket as though she were holding onto a life-jacket.

Because he had never looked at her like that before. As man to woman. For many years she had secretly wanted him to, but now that it was happening she found it curiously unsettling. And insulting.

'Oh, for heaven's sake, Nick!' she snapped angrily. 'I know that ogling women probably comes as easily to you as breathing—but it isn't really an appropriate time to ogle me, is it? Or have you always found widows easy prey in the past?'

That hit home. But as soon as the words were out of her mouth Abigail regretted them, her heart sinking with some nameless fear as his mouth became an ugly line and the light of retaliation flared in his eyes. 'If we're talking *appropriate* behaviour,' he mocked, 'then I've yet to see your tears, Abigail, dear. I've rarely met a widow who was so composed. Or who showed quite so much of her beautiful, black-stockinged thighs.'

'It was the only black suit I had!' she said defensively.

'Which just happens to mould every sexy curve of that beautiful body?' he mocked, with cold laughter in his eyes.

'Any more of this and I'm getting out and walking,' she threatened, wondering if he had any inkling of just how her body was betraying her by responding to that erotic criticism.

'Not in those shoes, you aren't, sweetheart!' And the laughter was switched off as he glanced down at the delicate, black patent leather concoctions which were strapped around her narrow ankles. 'Unless you're planning to spend the rest of the day in the local casualty department, that is.' He gave her another appraisal, but this time there was none of the lazy approval which had made her heart race like a train. This time his eyes were impartial. And disapproving.

'What the hell have you been doing to yourself?' he demanded. 'Why are you so thin?'

Abigail glared. 'Most women in the western hemisphere are striving for cheekbones, Nick!' she retorted. 'Don't you know that you can never be too rich or too thin?'

'Slenderness should not equal unhealthiness,' he replied.

'I am *not* unhealthy!'

'No?' He turned her face towards him and cupped it in his strong, brown hand and Abigail felt, suddenly and frighteningly, terribly, terribly vulnerable. 'Then why are your cheeks so pale? Your face so pinched? I don't know about interesting hollows, Abigail— they're more like bloody great ravines in your case!' He let his hand drop.

'Orlando was an actor!' she said, as if that really mattered. 'And he liked me to look good!'

'A thin, pale, pretty little accessory—the compliant little doll,' he mused reflectively. 'So, no change there, then.'

'It wasn't *like* that!'

'No? Then why don't you tell me what it *was* like? Tell me about your relationship with Orlando.'

'No!' she declared heatedly, aware that he had unwittingly touched on the rawest nerve of all. 'Why on earth would I want to tell *you* anything?'

'Because confession is good for the soul, didn't you know that, Abby?' he purred, and now his green eyes were as watchful as a cat's. 'Wasn't marriage everything you dreamed it would be? Did the delectable Orlando fall in your expectations of him?'

And this, too, hit home—far more accurately and woundingly than he could ever have imagined. Abigail's mouth trembled violently, pain and anger overwhelming her as she met the mocking question in his eyes.

'You have no right to talk to me that way, Nick! To ask me questions like that! Especially not today,' she finished on a shudder.

His face was quite expressionless. 'Oh, but that is where you are wrong, Abby. I have every right,' he answered, with a smooth assurance which made her want to lash out at him.

She drew a deep breath. 'And why's that?'

'Because your stepfather trusted me. He appointed me executor of his will—'

'Nick,' interrupted Abigail. 'Philip died well over a year ago. You fulfilled all your obligations as executor then. I inherited Philip's estate—end of story. We are no longer bound by even the most tenuous of ties. We need never see each other again.'

'No, I don't suppose we do.' He gave her a long, considering look. 'But here I am.'

'Here you are,' she said dully, a sharp pang of apprehension overwhelming her as she tried to imagine never seeing him again.

There was silence in the car as it purred through the narrow, frosty lanes, and Abigail tried to tell herself that the unsettling feelings his appearance had provoked were simply a reaction to her husband's death. And a reminder of her youth, of simpler times, when the outside world had not seemed such a big and hostile place. Because I was cosseted and protected from it, Abigail recognised as she stared at the ploughed fields, where frost like icing sugar glittered thickly.

'What made you decide to sell all the shares that Philip left you?' asked Nick suddenly.

The question was so unexpected that Abigail started as though he had tipped icy water over her head. 'How did you know that?'

He gave her an impatient look. 'Oh, come on, Abby—I know you wouldn't exactly qualify as businesswoman of the year, but you can't be *that* naive! If shares are floated on the stock market, then it isn't exactly a state secret, is it?'

'N-no,' answered Abigail uncertainly. She would just as easily have ridden a rocket to the moon as been able to talk with any degree of knowledge on the subject of stocks and shares; she had left all that kind of thing to Orlando. Because that, more than anything, had kept him off her back. In more ways than one. A dull flush crept into her cheeks.

'It just surprised me, that's all,' said Nick, giving her a shrewd look. 'Just as it surprised me that you sold the New York apartment earlier in the year.'

Abigail tasted the bitter flavour of memory in her mouth, the utter chaos of the last year coming back to torment her. 'Yes, the New York apartment,' she echoed, in a hollow kind of whisper. 'Sold.'

'There's no need to sound so horrified.' Nick threw her a strange glance. 'You knew all about the sale, of course?'

'How could I not know?' she queried. 'It was *my* flat, wasn't it? And *my* inheritance.'

His dark, enigmatic face looked almost pitying. 'Poor little rich girl,' he murmured, and turned his dark profile to the car window to survey briefly the English winter landscape. The fat flakes of snow had multiplied and now there were whole armies of them, swirling down to settle on the iron-hard ground.

'In theory it was your inheritance,' he continued relentlessly. 'But when you married dear Orlando, of course, what was yours became his, and what was his became yours. That's what I love about marriage,' he added sarcastically. 'The total trust involved.'

'You cynical—'

'Not to mention the fundamental inequality of the equation,' he carried on relentlessly. 'Orlando got half your substantial fortune, and you got half Orlando's debts.' He gave her a bland smile. 'Or did you do the decent thing and get rid of them for him? It's *such* a strain to begin a marriage with money problems pressing down on you, wouldn't you say, Abby?'

'Shut up!' she yelled heatedly, turning in times of stress to the simple insults of their youth. 'Just shut up, will you?'

'Make me,' he suggested softly.

She did not see the danger in his challenge. 'Too right I will!' Abigail lunged at him, hurling herself across the back seat of the car to land half on top of him, with her hands curled up into tiny fists.

She hit him over and over again, pummelling at the solid wall of his chest, calling him every name under the sun, scarcely aware of what she was doing or saying, until at last he captured both hands in one large, firm hand and held them away from him. She became suddenly aware that her face was very close to his, and that her heart was pounding inside her head. And that his lips were parted, almost as if…as if…

The flicker of desire she felt was immediately obliterated by despair and Abby quickly shut her eyes. When she opened them again it was to find Nick staring down at her repressively, still grasping her hands tightly within his.

'That's enough, Abby,' he told her sternly. 'Understand? Enough!'

She shook her head, the thick, honey-coloured hair swaying wildly. 'No! It is not enough!' she retorted, her voice cracking with the strain of the last few days…the last few months… 'Oh, God, Nick…Nick…'

'I know,' he said quietly. 'It's all right, Abby. I know.'

'No, you don't!' she wailed, as the memory of her marriage slammed home to crush her spirit yet again. 'You can't possibly know! No one can!'

'I know that you need to cry,' he told her, softly and very deliberately, and drew her into his arms. 'I know that if you bottle it up much longer, then you'll explode.'

'Oh, Nick,' she moaned, and, burying her face in his immaculate shoulder, Abigail dissolved into helpless, sobbing tears.

CHAPTER TWO

ABIGAIL did not move her head away from Nick's shoulder, and he let her cry until there were no tears left, until her sobs became dry, exhausted gasps.

He took a large, beautifully pressed handkerchief from his pocket and silently handed it to her, but her hands were trembling so much from the flood of raw emotion that she could barely hold onto it. Abigail waved his hand away distractedly.

'Here,' he said, frowning. 'Let me.' His touch was almost gentle as he pushed stray strands of hair from her wet cheeks and then dried the tears away.

Abigail felt foolish and vulnerable. And Nick was the last person in the world she would have chosen to witness her breaking down in a full flood of hysterical tears.

'Better now?' he queried, after a moment or two.

'Yes. Thank you.'

'Then let's go.' Nick rapped on the smoked-glass panel which divided them from the driver, and it was only then that Abigail noticed the car had pulled over onto the side of the road.

'W-why did we stop?' she sniffed as the car pulled away.

'I didn't think that you'd want an audience while you wept,' he said matter-of-factly. 'And certainly not

31

an audience consisting of that crowd up at the house,'
he added disparagingly.

Abigail blew her nose rather more noisily than
usual. 'They're Orlando's friends,' she objected
automatically, more because it was the habit of a lifetime, objecting to anything Nick said, rather than because she actually disagreed with him.

'And yours?' he quizzed softly. 'Are they your
friends, too?'

Abigail looked at him. 'Not really, no.'

'Oh?'

Abigail was beginning to discover that he was
simply not the kind of man you could reproach for
asking deeply personal questions—that was the trouble. Was it because he had known her for most of her
life that he felt he had the right to probe? Or did he
ask *all* women questions like this? 'They're not my
type.'

He nodded his head, as though her answer came as
no surprise to him. 'I see.' He glanced down at his
shoulder to find a stray, glistening tear, and he ruefully brushed it away with one long finger.

The gesture touched her unbearably—but she didn't
for the life of her know why. And so that she wouldn't
make a fool of herself yet again, by blubbing all over
him, Abigail said the first mundane thing which came
into her head. 'I'm sorry about your jacket.'

'It's just a jacket.' He shrugged.

'I'll have it cleaned—'

'Oh, for heaven's sake!' he interrupted grimly.
'Stop talking as though we had just met at a cocktail

party! I think I preferred you shouting and punching me to that.'

She smiled at the exasperation on his face; for the first time in days she actually smiled. And then her heart missed a beat as his exasperation turned into a brief smile which matched hers.

'I must look a sight,' she said automatically.

Green eyes scanned her face, but the smile had disappeared and irritation had replaced it. 'A bit,' he answered tersely. 'Your face is all blotchy and it's obvious you've been crying.'

'Gee—thanks,' she answered drily. 'When I need a boost in confidence, remind me to avoid you like the plague!'

'Just what is it with you, Abby?' he demanded softly. 'You're supposed to be playing the grieving widow, not a flaming fashion model! Can't you function properly unless you know you're looking beautiful?'

She gazed at him in amazement, more at the fact that Nick, *Nick*, had paid her some kind of compliment—even if it *was* a backhanded one!—than at his tone of voice. 'Beautiful?'

He made a clicking sound of impatience. 'Sorry,' he said in a bored voice, leaning back carelessly against the seat and staring into space, 'but I'm not playing that game.'

'What game?' she asked, genuinely confused.

His voice changed into a parody of a woman gushing. 'Oh, heavens, Nick—surely you don't think that I'm *beautiful*!' His eyes hardened as his gaze roved over the pale oval of her face. 'Particularly when the woman in question has the kind of face which could launch a thousand ships, if you'll excuse the somewhat hackneyed expression.'

She didn't have the energy to row. 'Let's drop it, shall we?'

'With pleasure. Anyway, we're here.' Nick turned to glance out of the window as the car made its way up the sweeping gravel-drive towards the handsome Georgian house which she and Orlando had bought just after their marriage. They drove through the impressive gardens which were flanked by vast yew tunnels, and a flash of afternoon sunlight glinted off the distant lake.

Through the windows of the lighted drawing-room, Abigail could see people opening bottles and bottles of champagne, and she mentally steeled herself to confront them, wishing that she could order them out of her house and have the place to herself again. Time to lick her wounds and recover.

But tomorrow they would all be gone, she reminded herself. Tomorrow she would have the peace she craved.

'It's strange,' Nick remarked as the car drew to a halt with a soft, swishing sound, 'but I never imagined that you would end up living in a big, impressive pile in the English countryside, out in the middle of nowhere like this.'

'Orlando wanted to,' she found herself telling him. 'And I liked it here, too,' she added defensively.

His gaze was unwavering. 'And did Orlando always get what Orlando wanted?'

Did he know? Had he somehow guessed? Was that the reason for the piercingly direct gaze which seemed perceptive enough to be able to read her mind? Abigail shuddered violently as shame and revulsion washed over her. There was no point in denying what was as obvious as the nose on her face. 'He did, mostly,' she managed. 'He was well schooled in the art of persuasion, you know.'

'Yes. So I believe.' Nick looked down at her pale hands, knotted together and lying against the black skirt. 'Abby, you're trembling.' He sounded appalled. 'What on earth is the matter with you?'

She settled for her only credible source of defence. 'Need you ask? It's been a fraught day. A fraught week. And I'm not particularly looking forward to going in there and mingling with people I don't even like.'

'Then don't do it.'

She gave him a sad little smile. 'I can't just opt out like that.'

'Can't you?' he queried softly. 'You can do whatever you want to do, you know.'

'Only if your name happens to be Nick Harrington,' came her dry response. 'And we don't all have your determination.'

This received the glimmer of a smile. 'Come on,' he said, and helped her out of the car with an old-fashioned courtesy which she was quite unused to. It had the effect of making her feel very warm and safe and secure. A girl could get used to being cosseted like this, thought Abigail with a wistfulness which was totally alien to her.

Her instincts had always taught her to be wary where this man was concerned, but instinct also told her that nothing could ever harm her while Nick was around. In a topsy-turvy world, he had a rare strength and constancy of character.

She watched him as he slammed shut the door of the limousine behind them and they slowly began to mount the pale blonde stone of the front steps.

Nick Harrington would, she thought, with a sudden, unwelcome pang of realisation, make some woman one hell of a husband.

They had almost reached the front door when she stopped and turned to face him. 'You always give me such a hard time, Nick—'

'Do I?'

'You know you do. You always have done.'

'You need someone to say no to you, Abby. You've had a whole lifetime of people spoiling you, giving you exactly what you want.'

'No,' she corrected. 'People giving me what *they* wanted me to have. It isn't the same thing at all.'

Was that understanding which momentarily glimmered in the verdant depths of his eyes? On an impulse she placed her hand on his forearm. 'Thank you for coming today,' she told him honestly, because right at that moment he seemed the only solid, familiar shape in her quicksand-shifting world. 'I appreciate it. Really, I do.'

He nodded as she let her arm fall but, far from looking gratified at receiving possibly the first compliment she had ever paid him, his face was grim and unyielding. 'Don't speak too soon, sweetheart,' he said ominously, turning the door handle and pushing it open.

And Orlando's friends were suddenly flocking around them, like vultures at a carcass, before Abigail had a chance to ask him exactly what he meant.

In Ireland the post-funeral party was known as a wake, though Abigail had often wondered why, since, judging from the facial expressions of most of the people here today, they looked about as *un*awake as she could imagine. In fact, a few of them looked just about ready to pass out.

She did what little mingling was necessary, but the effort it took must have shown on her face, for Nick soon came to stand beside her; he frowned, and then dipped his dark head to say in an undertone, 'Why don't you sit down? Take the weight off your feet.'

She didn't know why she found it so difficult to follow suggestions when they were made by Nick— but she did. She always had done. And yet what he said made sense. Come on, Abby, she reasoned with herself, stop beating yourself up.

'Okay.' She nodded, and sat down stiffly in one of the high-backed chairs, forcing herself to sip from a glass of champagne, but pushing aside the untasted smoked salmon sandwiches on the place beside her, which were already curling up at the edges.

She drank the whole glass down, thinking that it might make her feel better, but by the end of it she felt resoundingly and head-achingly sober, though everyone else was well away, quaffing like mad at the vintage brand which Orlando had always preferred as though it were going out of fashion.

Nick had, in effect, she thought gratefully, now taken on the role of host. Abigail had barely been able to string two sentences together since they had returned—to find the party in full swing.

'Do you want me to get rid of them?' he asked her softly as they listened to one of Orlando's buddies from drama school telling an outrageous story about her dead husband.

'Soon,' she answered.

Nick winced as the teller reached the predictably lewd and lascivious punchline, which was greeted with raucous laughter. 'Doesn't that kind of talk about your husband bother you?' he asked her curiously.

Oh, what little he knew! Abigail shook her head. 'Very little bothers me these days,' she answered calmly, thanking a benevolent God that Orlando's elderly parents, living in Spain because it was a kinder climate for people with chest problems, had been considered too frail and in too much shock to attend their son's funeral.

'Some of these people have come a long way to be here today, Nick,' she explained quietly as she met his bemused stare. 'Let them have their fill of food and drink. I need never see any of them again.'

He raised dark, quizzical eyebrows. 'That bad, huh?'

She nodded her head reluctantly, the thick hair feeling hot and heavy against her neck. 'That bad. So let them feel free.'

And they felt free, all right. The trouble was that they seemed like bottomless pits where the alcohol was concerned. Abigail was seriously concerned that, any minute now, someone would completely disgrace themselves. I really ought to go and ask the caterers to start serving coffee, she thought tiredly, unable to summon up the energy to move as she watched the guests group and regroup, dark dramatic figures, swaying more and more as each second passed.

Jemima, the dark, elfin-looking creature, with stray feathers from the feather boa sticking tantalisingly to her scarlet lips, was behaving quite outrageously—even for a member of Orlando's entourage.

She made a beeline for Nick as soon as she spotted him, and then tried to drape herself all over him.

Abigail observed him with wry amusement as he politely attempted to keep her at arm's length. His body language spoke volumes! Surely even Jemima must be able to sense that he was not in the least bit interested in her?

Apparently not. Jemima let a wing of raven hair fall provocatively over one half of her face, and looked up at Nick with huge dark eyes, blurred by alcohol. 'Are you Abigail's lover?' she slurred.

Abigail held her breath as she waited for his reaction. There had been plenty of women in his life. He was a man of the world, and, naturally, she imagined that he must be terribly liberal and unshockable. Well, he certainly looked shocked now. Shocked *and* outraged! Abigail was amazed.

'I beg your pardon?' he queried icily.

Jemima clearly had a thick skin. 'I just sh-shaid,' she mumbled. 'Are you getting it on? With Abigail?'

Suddenly the room went completely still. Curious, debauched-looking faces were turned with avid interest towards the tall man in the elegant dark suit.

Not a flicker of emotion stirred the breathtakingly handsome features, and yet his face was somehow all the more threatening for its complete lack of expression. Abigail thought that it was like looking at a cold, glittering mask of a man's face.

'Abigail buried her husband today,' Nick told Jemima with frosty disdain. 'And even if *you* don't have a breath of decency in your body, then at least you might show *her* a little respect.'

His eyes became stormy, and Abigail saw that those strong, capable hands had clenched into fists beside the powerful shafts of his thighs. Quickly she looked away again.

'Perhaps you would like to apologise to her before you leave?' he suggested stonily.

'Apologise?' Jemima's voice was shrill and she shot Abigail a malicious stare. 'Apologise for what? For stating the truth? Come on, darling—everyone knows that Abigail and Orlando had a very *open* marriage. In the truest sense of the word,' she finished, with a suggestive little pursing of her big, glossy lips.

For a moment Abigail met Nick's appalled eyes over the top of Jemima's head. She saw the bleak, disbelieving question written there, before his mouth thinned with distaste and he said, quite firmly, 'The party's over, folks, I'm afraid. And I'd like you all to leave.'

Jemima was still staring at Abigail, but the spite which was spitting from her eyes had now evolved into pure jealousy. 'Sure we'll leave,' she drawled. 'And we wish you all the luck in the world—you'll need it! Orlando always said that going to bed with Abigail was like sleeping with an ice-cube!'

Abigail started as though she had been stung.

Like a child trying desperately not to cry, she crammed her fist into her mouth, as if to halt the bitter words of denial. She wanted to move, to run, to hide, to scream, but she felt powerless and heavy, as though the blood in her veins had turned to stone. She was trapped. Paralysed with fear. She made a tiny cry at the back of her throat, like that of a wounded animal, and she saw, from his look of fury, that Nick had heard the pitiful little sound.

'Get *out* of here!' he snarled, and the anger on his face subdued every person present. He took a slow, menacing step towards Jemima, who was staring up at him in horror, as if unused to the full brunt of a truly masculine rage.

'Yes, *you*,' he emphasised to Jemima in disgust, before turning to face the rest of them. 'And all you others! You greedy, grasping pathetic bunch of parasites! You can take your nasty little stories and your freeloading ways and your sordid little lives and get out of here. *Now!*'

The strangely subdued gathering needed no second bidding. Glasses were hastily put down and they began to scuttle out, like children chastised by the headmaster.

It took about five minutes for the room to empty, leaving only the priest and two white-aproned waitresses, who stood looking up at Nick with a kind of nervous respect. The priest hastily said a polite farewell and left.

'Did you mean for us to go, too, sir?' one of the waitresses asked tentatively.

And Abigail then witnessed the most astonishing transformation.

Nick turned to the two women with a wide, apologetic smile and a rueful shake of his dark head. 'No, of course I didn't mean for you to go, too,' he said. 'And I'm sorry if you thought I did. I just thought that things had gone quite far enough—'

'Oh, they *had*, sir!' piped up the other. 'They had! And you did absolutely right to say what you did! We was just saying in the kitchen—never heard language *like* it in our lives! Especially at a *funeral*! Absolutely disgusting!'

Nick glanced over at Abigail, who was still sitting motionless on the stiff-backed chair. 'I just didn't want Mrs Howard distressed any more—'

And suddenly Abigail could bear it no longer. Was Nick an actor, just like Orlando? Able to switch his emotions on and off at will, like a tap? One minute ejecting forty people from a room by the sheer force of his will and the next oozing so much charm that he had two middle-aged women positively eating out of his hand.

Jumping out of the chair, she stumbled towards the door. The older of the two waitresses tried to halt her.

'Miss—'

The careworn arm she placed on Abigail's arm was comforting and, Abigail supposed, reassuring, too. But she was still too disturbed to do anything other than shake it off distractedly. 'Let me go,' she pleaded, on a harsh gasp which seemed to be torn from somewhere deep inside her. 'Please! Let me go!'

'It's all right,' she heard Nick tell them, in a clipped and decisive voice. 'Mrs Howard will be fine. Please let her go.'

CHAPTER THREE

ABIGAIL ran out of the room and directly up the staircase which rose from the inner hall, her laboured breathing sounding loud and distorted in the almost eerie silence which had settled on the house.

She did not go to hers and Orlando's bedroom; she had not slept there for months.

But it was a magnificent room, overlooking the house's greatest glory—its eighteenth-century garden—and Abigail had half thought that she might move back in, once the policeman had told her that Orlando was never coming home again.

But now she knew that nothing would ever entice her to sleep in that room again.

Instead, she made her way to the East Room, whose curtains were drawn almost shut, leaving only a chink in the heavy brocade, giving the bedroom a gloomy half-light which suited her mood perfectly.

With a sense of relief, she kicked off the spindly high-heeled shoes, unbuttoned her black jacket and lay down on the wide four-poster bed, staring sightlessly up at the ceiling.

In the distance she could hear the faint chink of china and glass being clattered, and supposed that the waitresses were clearing away the debris from the food.

Time ticked by slowly, and she wondered where Nick was. Then she had to ask herself whether she had honestly expected him to come chasing up the staircase after her.

Not really.

Nick admired control, a quality which he possessed in abundance. Doubtless her hysterical departure in front of the waitresses would have had him shuddering with distaste; he had probably decided to leave her to get on with it until she had calmed down.

The thought also occurred to her that he might already have left with the others, and this thought, for some reason, absolutely filled her with horror.

But no. She gave her head a little shake. Nick would not have left; instinct told her that. They had never been bosom buddies, true, but they went back a long, long way. He had obviously come to the funeral out of a sense of loyalty. And, however disgusted he might be feeling by what had taken place, however soon he wanted to leave—and she couldn't blame him for that—she knew that he wouldn't go without saying goodbye.

Not Nick.

Her eyelids felt as though they had been weighted with lead, and she allowed them to drift over her sore eyes.

She would shut them briefly. Just for a moment.

Her head relaxed against the feather-softness of the pillow and darkness thankfully obliterated memory.

When she opened her eyes again the room was almost dark, but something in her surroundings had changed.

Nothing visibly different, but there was now a sound which had not been there before. Faint, almost imperceptible, and yet remarkably familiar.

There it was again.

She listened, then turned her face towards the window to find that Nick was sitting in the tall tapestry chair which stood in front of the luxurious gold and blue curtains, his eyes masked by the dim lamplight in the room. Beside him, on a small table, was a tray of tea.

They stared at one another for a long moment in silence, and Abigail realised that the sound she had heard was the sound of his breathing, soft and regular and even.

He wordlessly got up from the chair and came and sat on the side of the bed. He lifted a thick strand of the honey-coloured hair between his fingers, then let it fall again, spilling down, strand by shiny strand, to gleam like gold against the bleached backdrop of the pillow.

Still not completely awake, Abigail blinked up at him through thick, dark lashes. What the hell was he doing?

She wondered if the confusion showed in her eyes as she gazed at him, searching for something neutral to say—not words which would stir up the whole ghastly scene of earlier.

And then he did something extraordinary.

Leaning forward, just a fraction, he slowly traced

the outline of her lips, and they trembled violently beneath his fingertip.

Her eyes widened with shock and pleasure. She was completely at a loss to know why he had done such a thing. 'Nick—'

'Shh.' His voice was all velvet and cream—soft and rich and irresistible—and almost as tantalising as that leisurely touch, which to all intents and purposes was as innocent as could be.

So why was it making her heart beat so loud that she was certain he must be able to hear it? And why was every nerve-ending in her body screaming out for something more than that seemingly innocuous connection between fingertip and mouth?

She found her gaze raking hungrily at the hard, shadowed planes of his face, at the grass-green eyes— more secretive and mysterious than she could ever remember seeing them. Admit it, Abigail, she told herself. You want Nick Harrington. You want him now. The way you've always wanted him.

Caught up in the powerful net of desire, Abigail was spellbound, unable to move, to speak, to do anything other than stare up into that formidably handsome face.

He moved a little closer, so that his head was directly above hers, and he was looking down at her with narrowed eyes which were far from friendly. Not friendly, no, but intense. Burning with intensity.

This was getting out of hand. In her heart she knew that she must do something to stop it before it went any further.

'Nick…' she said again, but this time he silenced her with his lips.

Abigail had had laughably little experience with men. She had been kissed by a ski-instructor when she was sixteen, and then, almost two years later—by Orlando.

And Orlando had been experienced. Oh, yes. Orlando had kissed with the confidence and technique of a man who had kissed a *lot* of women before, who knew just about everything there was to know on the subject of kissing.

But this was so different.

Nick coaxed her lips apart with nothing more than the warm, soft pressure of his mouth—as though her mouth was some erotic new territory he was intent on exploring in the slowest and most delectable way possible.

She could never remember feeling so alive, or so compliant, or relaxed. Or excited. Her mouth opened even as her eyelids were drifting down to blot out the reality of who was kissing her—the heady pleasure making it terribly easy to ignore the nagging questions in her mind.

She sighed out her pleasure, and whether Nick felt it, or heard it, Abigail did not know. All she *did* know was that he chose that moment to deepen the kiss, moving his tongue inside her mouth with provocative precision, to circle it against the roof of her mouth in what seemed like the ultimate in erotic invasion.

She let her hands drift up to his shoulders, loving the feel of the honed muscles there, and instinctively she pulled him right down on top of her, revelling in the hard, lean weight of him, loving the possessive feeling of his hands as they reached out to entwine themselves in the heavy silk of her hair.

The kiss went on and on; Abigail had no idea for how long, because time had become a distant, forgotten concept in his arms. She had never known that a kiss could be so…so unbelievably arousing. All the tension and sorrow and confusion she had felt was disappearing by the second, eroded by the magic of that kiss.

Inside she was melting, unfurling, and her limbs began to stir with a vague, restless longing that made her long to say his name aloud, to plead with him to do something more. But she did not dare. She just entwined her arms tightly around his neck and felt the warm thrill of triumph as she heard his harsh shudder of capitulation.

It was then that it started to go wrong.

Abigail could pinpoint the moment exactly.

It was when he started to unbutton the soft white silk shirt she wore beneath the black jacket. Her body reacted to such intimacy before her brain had a chance to analyse it. She was holding her breath in sheer delight at the wonder of anticipation, feeling her nipples peak and scrape against the delicate lace of her confining bra.

It was only when he freed the second button, and she felt the faintly cooling rush of air washing over her lace-covered breasts, that the instinct born of experience made Abigail tense up.

He sensed it immediately—he must have done—for without warning he thrust her away from him, a dark, furious look of censure on his face as he stared at her with disbelief before levering himself off the bed.

Still breathing heavily, he strode over to the window and hoisted back the heavy brocade. Outside it was dark and starless. Only a cloud-blotted moon, almost full, loomed up out of the indigo sky to mock them with its inane, smiling face.

And only when his breathing had steadied down to something approaching normal did he say, in stark accusation, 'So it's true, then.'

Abigail's hands were trembling. She couldn't even think about what he was saying until she had got rid of the damning evidence of what had almost just happened. And that meant doing her shirt up. But she was so het up that even this simple task seemed beyond her. Her fingers slithered and skated all over the silky material, and it took an inordinate amount of concentration before she was able to slip the errant buttons back into their holes.

Running her hands back through her mussed hair, she forced herself to sit up on the bed and said to his back, 'What's true?'

He turned round then, and Abigail wished that he hadn't, for the intense disgust and…and…disappointment on his face was breathtaking.

He shook his head in disbelief. 'I thought that woman downstairs was about as low as a person could sink,' he said bitterly, almost to himself. 'Except that now I discover a few unwelcome home truths about myself.'

Abigail swung her legs over the side of the bed and pushed her protesting feet back into the ridiculously spindly shoes. She somehow felt less undressed with her shoes on. She cleared her throat, trying not to sound nervous, but nervous she was. And guilty, too. 'What are you talking about, Nick?'

'I was talking about me—which is really beside the point,' he said, in a dangerous whisper of self-disgust. 'About my unwelcome and rather pagan desire to have you writhing beneath me on that bed right now—'

It was shocking only because his words echoed her own burning wish—she *wanted* to be beneath him on that bed. Writhing. Kissing. 'Nick, don't—' she whispered, appalled.

'But let's not talk about *me*. Why don't we talk about *you* instead, Abby?' he carried on relentlessly, as if she hadn't spoken. 'And my over-the-top, ridiculously chivalrous defence of your honour downstairs—heavens, how Orlando's rather questionable friends must have been laughing behind their hands. Because now it's pretty clear to me that dear Jemima obviously spoke the truth—didn't she?' His green eyes glittered like costly emeralds. 'So tell me, Abigail, just how ''open'' was this open marriage of yours? If I had turned up, say, a month ago, would it have been just as okay to have seduced you on that bed over there?'

'You didn't seduce me.'

'No,' he agreed slowly. 'I stopped. Didn't I?'

Abigail clasped her palms up to her flaming cheeks in horror. 'Don't,' she whispered again.

'Don't what?' he mocked. 'Don't tell the truth? Don't be honest? But I thought that was the whole rationale behind ''open'' marriages. And you still haven't answered my question, have you? Would you have let me make love to you when Orlando was alive? Perhaps he would like to have watched? Hmm? Would he? Was that how you both got your kicks, Abby?'

'You're disgusting—'

'Well, maybe I am,' he admitted, his mouth curving with dislike and self-recrimination. 'But at least I'm not a hypocrite. Dear Lord, you looked so shocked downstairs, when Jemima accused you, that I was seriously worried you might faint right away—like some innocent Victorian heroine.' He gave a derisory laugh. 'When in reality you couldn't wait to get upstairs and start grappling on the bed with the nearest man!'

'Is that what you think of me?' she asked him steadily.

He gave her a cool look. 'What else am I supposed to think? People tend to get judged on how they behave, and your behaviour today has done nothing to disprove what Jemima said downstairs.'

Abigail clenched her fingernails into her palms so hard that she winced from the pain, but she didn't care. She didn't have to stay and listen to his insults. The easiest thing in the world would be to run from the room, away from his vile accusations, and the memory of the squalid little scene which had taken place here.

But running away would not do.

Nick would leave and carry with him that enduring memory of her as some cheap little tramp, who was completely at home with Orlando's friends and ready to embrace all their repugnant values.

She could not bear him to think that of her; she simply could not bear it. And it wasn't just a question of pride. She owed it to the stepfather who had given her so much love, and whom Nick, too, had idolised, to disabuse him of the awful impression she must have made.

'Nick,' she began tentatively.

His face was stony cold. He swept a disdainful look over her. 'What?'

She sighed, accepting that there was no easy way to say this. 'Look, I'd like to explain…'

'Should make interesting listening,' he said sarcastically.

'My marriage wasn't happy…'

But he interrupted her by throwing back his dark head and laughing, as cynical and as disillusioned a laugh as she had ever heard. 'Really?' he queried mockingly. 'You *do* surprise me, Abigail. I would have thought that indiscriminate couplings would have been the perfect recipe for matrimonial harmony!'

Her patience was being stretched to breaking-point, but Abigail was determined to continue until she had

made her point. Anything to get rid of that frighteningly cold look of disapproval in his eyes. 'Just because it wasn't happy, doesn't mean to say it was
"open", as you keep saying!' she snapped.

'So you were both faithful within the marriage?' he
countered immediately.

Flustered, she looked down and began to finger the
fine black wool of her skirt, rubbing it between finger
and thumb in the way that a child rubs a security
blanket. 'It—it isn't quite as easy as that,' she pre-
varicated.

'Oh, I think it is.' His voice sounded hard. 'Just
answer yes or no. It couldn't be simpler.'

With her forefinger, she drew an agonised circle on
the pale palm of her hand. How much to tell him?

She lifted her chin to meet his critical green gaze
and her dark blue eyes were unwavering. 'I was faithful,' she admitted, praying that he would not cotton
onto the reason for the pain which had darkened her
eyes.

His mouth was contemptuous. 'And you expect me
to believe that?'

Abigail shook her head, her patience beginning to
crumble. 'I don't expect you to do anything, Nick!'
she returned. 'But you might at least show me the
courtesy of hearing me out!'

'Why should I bother hearing you out?' he queried
coolly. 'Isn't that rather a waste of time? I mean—
don't genetics come into it?'

Abigail froze. She knew what was coming, yet still
she said, 'Meaning?'' in a hoarse croak of a voice.

'That you are your mother's daughter,' he suggested softly. 'And as promiscuous as she was.'

It was not the outrageous insult it should have been. After all, Nick at least had the courage to voice what other people had whispered for years. And, while Abigail had loved her mother, she had not been blind to her faults.

In an unconsciously childlike gesture, she caught at a stray strand of hair and began to twirl it like a bright, shiny rope around her finger.

She could handle his accusation in two ways.

She could rant and rail and order him out of the house. Or she could do the adult thing and confront him head-on.

She stopped twiddling the strand of hair. 'I'm not going to deny that my mother had lovers during her marriage to Philip,' she said stiffly, but she could not stop the fierce flood of shame which scorched her pale cheeks. 'Everyone knew that.' She paused and looked him full in the face. 'Including Philip,' she added boldly, and waited for Nick's astonishment, but, to her surprise, there was none.

'Yes,' he agreed tonelessly.

'You knew?' she queried. 'That Philip was aware—?'

'That your mother cuckolded him?' He nodded his head, then gave an empty laugh. 'Oh, yes, Abigail— I knew that. Philip may have been richer, older and thoroughly besotted with her, but he was no fool.'

Some remnant, some longing from her past for the kind of complete and fulfilled family life she had always yearned for, yet had always been denied, prompted her to say, very quietly, 'But she had her reasons for what she did—honestly, Nick.'

'I'm sure she did,' he agreed in a wintry voice. 'Lust is usually top of the list of reasons for infidelity, isn't it?'

'Oh, Nick,' said Abigail sadly. 'Now who's talking in black and white? Philip was a wonderful man, but he was almost forty years older than my mother—'

'And that's supposed to make me feel sorry for her, is it?' he demanded. 'To make me understand her unfaithfulness—perhaps even to condone it? Is that what you think, Abigail?'

'I'm just trying to explain—'

'And no explanation is necessary.' He cut across her ruthlessly. 'Your mother *knew* that Philip was a relatively old man when she married him. She was broke and all alone in the world, and Philip was a very rich man who was offering her a lifetime's security in marriage!'

'And she was a young and vibrant and beautiful woman!' Abigail defended. 'With the normal desires of a woman of that age which Philip couldn't satisfy for her!'

'Then she should have married someone her own age who could fulfil those desires, shouldn't she? Instead of opting for the financial security and luxury which Philip was offering her!' returned Nick forthrightly. 'She went into that marriage with her eyes wide open. She traded her youth and her beauty for money. It was a fair trade—if only she had kept to her side of the bargain.' He gave her an odd kind of smile. 'You know what they say—you pays your money and you takes your choice.'

How could she argue with him, when secretly she agreed with every word he said? She remembered the awful tension in the house when her mother had been in the midst of one of her little intrigues—it had been one of the reasons why Abigail had been sent back to England, to boarding-school. Philip had insisted.

And, when she had returned to America in the long vacations, it had been Philip who had lavished on her all the love and attention she craved. In fact, Philip had been more of a mother to her than her own mother! She gave a weary sigh and rubbed at the back of her neck, trying to shift the dull, nagging ache which would not seem to leave her.

Nick was watching her, and the tired little movement seemed to stir him into life. He lifted the heavy silver teapot and began to pour two cups of steaming tea. Just seeing him do that made Abigail realise that she'd had barely anything to eat or drink for twenty-four hours.

He stood up and brought the cup over to her, and she looked down, startled to find a wafer-thin slice of lemon floating in the scented tea.

Abigail felt a tiny glow of pleasure—until she pulled herself up short. Just because he had remembered how she took her tea, it did not mean that she should fall all over him with gratitude! Am I still, she thought rather despairingly, that lost and lonely little girl? Craving the affection she had been denied by her beautiful but oh-so-shallow mother?

She took the cup from him. 'Thank you,' she murmured automatically, and then, frowning, she realised what she had just said, and fixed him with a belligerent expression. 'Why on earth am I thanking you?' she demanded, more to herself, than to him, 'when you've spent the last ten minutes insulting me?'

He gave her something that resembled a smile as he sat down and sipped his own tea. 'That's better,' he observed softly. 'I think I like you better as protagonist rather than as victim.'

She shrugged her narrow shoulders and sipped at her tea. 'I can't imagine why you're still here.'

'Can't you?'

She stared up at him, wide-eyed. Was he alluding to their lovemaking? Was he perhaps expecting…? She shook her head. 'No.'

The bone-china cup was halfway to his lips, and there was the slightest hesitation before he replaced the cup on the saucer. 'I'm amazed it took you so long to ask,' he murmured, and then a feral gleam entered his green eyes. 'Or did you imagine that I was simply hanging around? Hoping to finish off what we started earlier on the bed?'

It was terrifying how her body reacted immediately to the mocking, sensual taunt, as if that deep slumberous voice had twitched a string of desire, and she felt the prickling of her breasts, the honeyed pull that began somewhere deep in her womb. Under cover of her tightly closed lips, she allowed her tongue to moisten the parched roof of her mouth.

'Well?' he persisted.

Over the years Abigail's contact with Nick had been sporadic, but she knew him well enough to realise that what would infuriate him more than anything would be if she failed to react to his outrageous sentiments.

She might have had a disappointing and unsatisfactory marriage, but it was over. She was free of Orlando now. For a long time she had been shackled into staying with her husband because she had been petrified of what he might disclose to the world about her if she left him.

She did not have to take this kind of criticism—not any more. Instead, she was going to have to learn how to argue her corner! And, besides, when Nick was seated on the opposite side of the room, he was far less intimidating.

She curved her mouth into an appalled little bow. 'Finish...off what we started earlier?' she repeated slowly, in a suitably horrified voice. 'You make it sound like digging a flowerbed!' She shook her head reprovingly, so that the honey sweep of her hair swayed in a heavy curtain around her long neck. 'Good heavens, Nick—if that's the kind of line you use to get women into bed, then I suspect that your bedpost must be exceptionally bare of notches!'

But, to her fury, he didn't look in the slightest bit angry, merely amused.

'I've never actually been inclined to notch up my

"conquests", as a woman who uses as outdated a term as "notches" would probably call them,' he murmured softly. 'But then I've never been the kind of man to keep score—certainly not in my love-life. Do you, Abby?' Again, that rather feral and threatening glint lit his green eyes. 'Keep score? If so, perhaps we could have some fun breaking a few of your records, what do you say?'

If there was an invisible line between what was socially acceptable and what was not, then Nick Harrington had just crossed it. Putting her cup down with a clatter, Abigail jumped to her feet and glared at him.

'I have tried to be adult and reasonable today,' she told him heatedly. 'To treat your insults with the contempt they deserve. I have refused to allow myself to be enticed into losing my temper with you—although the temptation to do so would have tried a saint—but enough is enough, Nick!'

"It is?' he queried innocently.

'It most certainly is.' She forced herself to speak calmly, but it wasn't easy when he was looking at her legs like that, with a cool and easy appreciation—as if he had every right in the world to do so. What a cheek!

She took a deep breath. And told herself to remember, firmly, that whatever she might be feeling about Nick right now, she had to admit that she had been pleased to see him earlier. She could not deny that she had leaned on him today—both literally *and* figuratively. Perhaps if she said goodbye to him nicely, then he might forget that she had been lying on the bed and kissing him earlier. She was hoping against hope that one day *she* might be able to forget it, too.

'Thank you for coming here today,' she finished formally. 'I appreciate it, truly I do. And I know that—'

'What will you do?' he interrupted brutally.

Something in his tone, as well as in the force of his question, made Abigail feel momentarily at a loss. 'Do?' she queried.

'Yes, Abigail—*do*. An alien word to you, I know,' he mocked.

Still not understanding, she let her heavy lids fall to half obscure the inky blueness of her eyes. 'Do? What, *now*, you mean?'

'Not just now, no. Unless you have any specific ideas…' He gave a cynical laugh as his eyes flickered meaningfully back towards the bed. 'I meant tomorrow. Next week. Next year. The future, Abby—the *future*.'

It was a word which had always frightened her—a word she had not allowed herself to consider. 'I— d-don't know.' Where was all this supposed to be leading? The tension had crept down her neck and was currently knotting her shoulders. In an effort to ease the strain, she raised her arms above her head and stretched.

Nick sat watching her, observing the movement with the hostile and silent fascination of a bird of prey. 'You still haven't answered my question,' he commented.

'I hadn't really thought about my plans, to be honest.' Which was true. For so long now she had been living minute by minute; things were somehow more bearable that way. She hunted around for inspiration and it came in the form of escape. 'I might go abroad,' she told him. 'To Paris, perhaps. Or Rome.'

'To do what?'

Abigail shrugged rather helplessly, given that those green eyes were fixing her with such a piercingly direct stare. 'To enjoy what those cities have to offer. What else?'

He did not look merely unimpressed—he looked positively disapproving. 'And then what?'

She frowned. 'What is this, Nick—the Spanish Inquisition?'

'I'm curious, Abby. Humour me. Then what?'

'Oh, I don't know!' she answered crossly. 'I'll wait and see what turns up.'

'Or *who* turns up, I suppose?' he suggested insultingly.

Abigail sucked in a long, indignant breath. 'You obviously *want* me to slap you around the face,' she fired at him boldly. 'And you're about five seconds away from having your wish granted!'

He acknowledged her taunt with a sardonic twist of his mouth, before continuing his assault. 'So are you intending to replicate your mother's life? Live in luxury off a series of men?'

'But I don't have to live off men!' she retorted triumphantly. 'I'm self-sufficient, remember? A woman of independent means.' She felt the urge to hurt him as much as he had hurt her with his comments. 'Philip left me his fortune—remember? And that's the reason you really dislike me, isn't it, Nick? Because before my mother and I came along *you* were the apple of Philip's eye. It was *you* that he would have left his money to. But he didn't, did he? And you've never really forgiven me for that, have you, Nick?'

There was a moment's silence and then, most peculiarly, given the circumstances, a smile of cold triumph began to lift the corners of his mouth.

'Strange, really,' he mused.

Something in his demeanour unsettled her. 'What is?'

'That in all your professed plans for the future you didn't mention what to most people would have been a priority—getting a job.'

Abigail stared at him as though he were mad. 'But I'm not really…qualified…to do anything—not really. You know that.'

The look he gave her was not a nice look. 'Yes, Abby, I know that. Your fancy boarding-schools and Swiss finishing school taught you nothing more than how to be a very decorative accessory, didn't they?' He let his gaze drift over her slender body. 'Although I must say that, although their horizons are obviously limited, they succeeded in what they set out to do. Because you certainly are very decorative. Very decorative indeed.'

Her pulse hammered with rage. Why should she stand here and put up with his criticism? she asked herself fiercely. And why should he go on about her getting a job in that high-handed way, as though it was the honourable thing to do? Especially when his words were motivated by an emotion as base as jealousy!

'Anyway,' she retorted, and something in his eyes made her defiant, made her *want* to shock him, 'why should I get a job? I don't want one—and I don't particularly need one. After all,' she added, forcing herself to smile a victorious smile as she attempted to rub salt into the wound, 'I have all the money I could ever need, don't I?'

She was aware now of the triumph in *his* smile, but it was a cold, oddly dangerous kind of triumph.

'I think you are very much mistaken,' he said quietly. 'As well as being very, very foolish.'

A solid little lump of fear had worked its way into her throat. 'What are you talking about?'

His green eyes were unwavering. 'What would you say, Abby,' he queried softly, 'if I told you that you didn't have a penny in the world?'

CHAPTER FOUR

ABIGAIL searched Nick's face, as if looking for a trace of humour in it, but there was none. Instead there was something cruel and implacable there.

And very, very scary.

'What the hell are you talking about?' she blustered.

'I'm talking about your finances!' he returned, with a quiet confidence which sent a little shiver of apprehension trickling down her spine. 'And it's a pity that you didn't do likewise—certainly while your husband was still alive!'

Something in his voice frightened her. 'What are you trying to tell me?'

'I'll put it to you very simply, just so that there can be absolutely no misunderstanding. Your money has gone, or rather it soon will be—'

'You're just trying to intimidate me!' she snapped, glancing around quickly at the solid comfort of the room, as if seeking reassurance that the ground she stood on was firm. This was surely just his over-the-top way of making some kind of point?

'And why should I want to do that?' he queried calmly.

'Because I know how much you hate me! But

enough is enough! I've just buried my husband, and even though…even though…' Her voice trembled.

'Even though what, Abby?' he prompted silkily.

'Even though you couldn't be bothered to shed a single tear at his graveside…'

She met his accusing gaze with a proud and steady stare. 'No, that's right! I couldn't! Because I am not like you, a hypocrite!' she returned quietly. 'I could not pretend to feel something which I didn't. And I didn't love Orlando!' She bit her lip until she tasted the warm salt of blood, and the release she felt was overwhelming as she admitted, 'I stopped loving him a long time ago…'

He let out a long, long sigh. 'Then why on earth,' he whispered softly, 'didn't you do something about it?'

She had expected some kind of self-congratulatory crowing, not that regretful understanding which had deepened his eyes to softest jade. Abigail stared at him, recognising again that his gentleness was powerful enough to coax her into confiding things that were probably best left unsaid.

'But I was,' she defended. 'I was doing something about it. I was going to get a divorce from Orlando. I was planning to see my solicitor just before he was…killed,' she finished on a gulp.

'And this dissatisfaction with the marriage. Just how long had that been going on?' he probed.

It was humiliating to have to admit defeat, especially to a man who would glory in it. 'Since almost the very beginning,' she admitted reluctantly.

'Then why didn't you act sooner?' he demanded. 'I'm certainly not into divorce just for the sake of it, if it happens to be a let-out just because a couple aren't getting along temporarily, but you were outrageously young when you married, and there were no children, thank God. A divorce would not have posed a huge problem, surely?'

She shook her head. Less of a problem than he would ever guess in a million years, but she would never tell him why. There were some things she could never tell anyone. Especially not Nick. 'I had my...reasons,' she responded stiffly, acutely aware that her high rise in colour must give away her discomfort, 'which I would prefer to keep to myself.'

For a moment he looked at the stubborn set of her chin, and then he let out an angry snarl, like a hungry lion left caged too long. He stormed over to the window and flung it wide open, inhaling a great breath of the cold night air and exhaling again deeply so that it left his lungs in great smoky streams.

Abigail watched him in amazement, this highly uncharacteristic display sending all other thoughts skittering from her mind.

Nick was the control freak—the man who never let his feelings show. Yet when she analysed his actions today, well, she had never seen him behave in quite such an emotional way. And Nick in a rage was rather endearing, she admitted to herself reluctantly as her eyes travelled over the lean, hard length of his body, now all tense and tight with rage. Endearing *and* sexy.

Oh, Lord, thought Abigail desperately, I don't *want*

to feel this way about him. To be so aware of him that it takes every ounce of self-control I possess not to go over to him and hurl myself into his arms and beg him to kiss me like he kissed me last time. She stared down at her clasped hands and wondered what he would say or do next.

But by the time he had shut the window he seemed to have gained something of his usual restraint. 'I should have stopped you from marrying him,' he said, almost to himself.

'But you tried, remember?' she reminded him acidly. 'The night before the wedding, as I recall. When you failed to make me—'

'See sense?'

She remembered how he had summoned her to him in that imperious way of his, and how she had sat stubborn and stony-faced while he had appealed to her common sense and her better nature, but to no avail. The marriage had taken place in spite of his entreaties. And all it would have taken to have stopped her from going through with it would have been one small sign that Nick cared...

She sighed, acknowledging the wisdom of hindsight—much as it would have pleased her to contradict him. She nodded. 'I guess so. I saw it as interference at the time.'

'Which it was. And necessary interference, as it turns out. *Damn!*' he swore loudly.

Abigail almost smiled. It was a long time since she had seen him so outwardly angry, and the passionate outburst gave her the courage to ask the question she had never dared to ask before. 'The night before the wedding, when you met with Orlando in the hotel, you—you offered him money not to marry me, didn't you?'

His head jerked up in surprise. 'Did he tell you that?'

So her intuition had been right! She shook her head. 'No. I guessed when he came back from his meeting with you. He had a kind of swagger about him...'

A triumphant swagger. How well she recalled the way he had strutted back into their room, looking flushed and exultant. He had ordered champagne and had then drunk rather too much of it for him to make sense as he had toasted their future together.

'But clearly not enough money,' Nick mused. 'My mistake in the whole affair was to underestimate Orlando. You see, I thought that his refusal of the money I offered him was an indication of how much he loved you. I thought that he could not be bought. Now, of course, I realise how wrong I was. He *could* be bought—if the price was right. I simply did not offer him enough.'

He gave a hollow laugh. 'Orlando recognised that the greatest riches lay not with my rather insulting offer to make him leave you alone but with his bride-to-be. His beautiful young heiress.' He looked directly down at her, the green eyes candid. 'And he was right, wasn't he, Abby? You were his passport to a life of indolence.'

She frowned, shaking her head distractedly, wishing that he would let it go.

'Because he never loved you, did he?' he demanded brutally.

Her glittering dreams had already been crushed underfoot, but surely some of them had once been shining and intact? Abigail tried to dredge up memories from the fog of her mind, tried to remind herself of Orlando when she had first met him, on a school skiing trip to France.

She had been a couple of months short of her eighteenth birthday, and *my* how he had impressed her. All bronzed and blond curls, with those bright blue eyes and that laughing, heady confidence which had all the girls flocking round him like bees around a honeypot.

But it had been *her* he had wanted, *her* he had sought out, with an extremely complimentary singlemindedness which had gone to her head. She had been young, lonely and idealistic. And ripe for his attentions.

At the time she had been flattered by his pursuit of her, but, during the long, lonely months of her failing marriage, she had forced herself to come to the conclusion that her meeting with Orlando had not been one of chance but rather manufactured by him.

Because she was rich.

And vulnerable.

'He never loved you, did he, Abby?' Nick persisted, and his clear green gaze captured hers, making it impossible for her to look away or to lie to him.

She tried to bury her head in her palms, but he moved swiftly across the room and caught her wrists, his dark hands easily encircling their narrowness. She felt the soft beat of her pulse begin to rise hectically beneath the roughened pads of his fingertips, and wondered if he could feel it, too.

'Look at me and admit it!' he demanded huskily. 'Admit that he didn't love you!'

'Why are you torturing me like this?' she asked him brokenly.

A muscle working furiously in one tanned cheek was the only sign that her remark had hit home. 'It isn't torture,' he insisted, although his voice softened a fraction. 'But I need you to be able to face up to the truth.'

She could not fight him any more. And, besides, only a remnant of redundant pride had prevented her from admitting it. Her blue eyes blazed sapphire fire at him. 'Okay, then, Nick—I'll tell you. Orlando never loved me! Never! He told me so after we were married...' She saw his look of outraged disbelief. 'Oh, not straight away. He waited...'

'Waited for what?'

She shook her head, swallowing down the lump of failure which was always ready to rise up and haunt her. 'That's...irrelevant.' She raked a handful of honey hair away from her face. 'So now you know! Does that satisfy you? Does that give you something to gloat about and make you say "I told you so"?'

He was still grasping her hands, she realised. He dropped his gaze briefly to the two slender wrists, with their fine sprinkling of golden freckles, before lifting his eyes to hers, and Abigail was taken aback by the profound sense of sadness in his expression as he relinquished his hold on her.

'Do you really think it gives me pleasure to have to drag that kind of admission from you? Do you?'

'I don't know!' Midnight-blue flames of confusion sparked in her eyes. 'Just tell me why you needed me to admit that Orlando never loved me?'

He grimaced. 'It might be better if we went downstairs to the study first. We might be more comfortable there, instead of standing facing each other like combatants.'

And then Abigail really was frightened. He sounded like a doctor about to break bad news... 'No,' she whispered. 'Tell me now.'

He shook his dark head. 'I asked the women who were helping downstairs to light a fire in the study before they left. This room isn't particularly welcoming. Come on, Abby, you're dead on your feet.'

She cursed his charm and persuasiveness even as she allowed herself to succumb to it. She nodded her head. 'Okay,' she whispered.

Narrowed green eyes surveyed her creased black suit and the fine silk stockings which encased her slender legs. 'Why don't you change into something more comfortable first?' he suggested.

Abigail raised her eyebrows. 'What's that—a cue to slip into some revealing little negligee?'

'Oh, such a cynic,' he observed softly, with something approaching regret in his voice. 'I'll wait for you downstairs in the study.'

He seemed to be forgetting that this was *her* house.

'There's no need to make it sound like I'm some naughty little schoolgirl being summoned into the headmaster's office!'

'That sounds more like your own particular fantasy rather than any valid objection, Abby,' he commented as he shot her a cool, analytical stare. 'Don't you think?'

She found that, no, she couldn't think, not after *that* remark. Or rather, she could. She started thinking about fantasies. About kissing Nick again. Only this time letting it go further. Just how much further would she let him go? Her heart thundered alarmingly in her chest. 'G-get out!' she spluttered.

'Oh?' He gave her a look of mocking disappointment before he disappeared, shutting the door behind him.

Abigail's hands were shaking after he had left, but she forced herself to think of the ghastly reality of sex, and that had the magic effect of banishing all these new and disturbingly erotic thoughts from her mind.

She slipped off the black jacket and draped it on the bed, a sense of foreboding creeping over her. He had said that her finances were in a mess—but just how bad could they actually *be*? And how could *he* possibly know anything about them?

She unzipped the pencil-line skirt and it dropped to the floor. She stepped out of it, just leaving it there in a crumpled black pool, knowing that she would never wear it again.

When she had married Orlando, she had wanted

them to be equal, and so, naturally, she had given him complete access to her money. And, then, when disillusionment had set in, the money had been the only defence she had to prevent his taunts, to maintain her sanity.

She unbuttoned her silk shirt and desperately tried to look on the bright side, pushing aside the memory of Nick's grim expression. After all, she reasoned, she had more than enough money to cope with an extravagant husband.

Okay, so he had sold the New York apartment, and he had got rid of a few shares, too. She knew that. But he had not been a fool, especially where money was concerned. He'd known that she was planning to see a lawyer with a view to getting a divorce, and that he would therefore be entitled to half her estate as a settlement. So he would hardly have put his own cause in jeopardy by frittering it all away, would he?

Abigail's cheeks burned as she stood clad in nothing but her underwear and stockings. Again she felt the tormenting scrape of tingling nipples against the lace of her bra as disturbingly erotic thoughts came flooding back to tantalise her.

Just what had happened to her earlier? she wondered. When she had awoken and Nick had come to her on the bed?

She had wanted him very badly—yes, she had. That was what had happened. She had kissed him back with uninhibited abandon, her mouth and her body demonstrating exactly how much she had wanted him.

She stifled a small, instinctive moan as she recalled

with uncomfortable clarity just how she had felt when Nick had started to unbutton her shirt. He had made her feel as though she were a delicious present he had been unwrapping.

In that one moment her desire for him had been overwhelming. And that in itself was a disturbing novelty.

Shivering, she went over to the huge wardrobe and scrabbled around inside, searching for clothes which would warm her. And, far more importantly, clothes which would protect her from the searing sensuality of that emerald gaze.

She peeled off and discarded her stockings, stepped into a pair of black jeans and pulled a warm pale grey sweater of softest cashmere over her head. Pushing her bare feet into a pair of soft black leather moccasins, she went downstairs to find him.

He was sitting in the study, scanning a newspaper, a log fire flaming by his side. To Abigail's surprise, he, too, had changed, into dark cords and a thick forest-green sweater, which looked like a handknit. Someone must love him very much to have spent hours knitting him a sweater like that, she thought, and an unwelcome spear of something which felt very much like jealousy shot through her.

He glanced up as she walked in, and gave her a brief, noncommittal smile. 'Come and sit down,' he said, and indicated the chair opposite him.

'Thanks,' said Abigail drily as she planted herself in the squashy leather chair. 'But there isn't any need to play host, thank you, Nick.' And then she remembered that she hadn't objected when he had filled that same role after the funeral. 'I'm sorry. That wasn't fair.'

'It doesn't matter.'

'Yes, it does. I was glad enough of your help earlier. Thanks.'

He frowned deeply as he watched her cheeks go pink. 'Please don't go all sweet on me, Abby. I'm not used to it, and it makes what I have to say that much more difficult.'

'Please just tell me what it is,' she urged quietly.

'Very well.' There was a pause. 'Today, when I mentioned that your New York apartment had been sold, you looked uncomfortable.'

'That's because I didn't particularly want to sell it.'

'Then *why* sell it?' he demanded.

Abigail sighed. 'Because Orlando thought that it was a waste of money. Which it was, in a way—I mean, we hardly ever used it.'

'It was also a very valuable piece of real estate,' he pointed out.

'So we made money from it!' she declared brightly.

He shook his dark head. 'Not very much. It was advertised for considerably below the market value, because Orlando wanted a quick sale.'

Abigail frowned in confusion. 'How do you know that?'

'Because I bought it.'

'*You* bought my flat?'

'That's right.'

'But *why*?'

He settled back in the chair, his hands clasped together, his two forefingers resting provocatively on the curve of his lower lip. 'Perhaps I wanted to make a quick buck?' he suggested.

'You're rich enough not to need to.'

'True,' he concurred, and his green gaze was steady. 'Okay, then, I bought it out of sentiment. Because it had been Philip's flat. And it *was* a bargain.'

'So the reality is that you ripped me off?'

He gave her a look of barely concealed impatience. 'What did you expect me to do? Go up to Orlando and say, Now look here—you're selling this flat too cheaply. Let me give you what I think it's really worth.'

He ran his hand through his dark hair, but the only result was that he successfully mussed it, to give him a just-got-out-of-bed look.

'Besides, you seem to be missing the point, Abigail—which is to ask yourself *why* Orlando should want such a quick sale. You might also ask yourself,' he added, 'why he has disposed of most of your shares and mortgaged this house up to the hilt?'

'M-mortgaged th-this house?' she queried, in a broken kind of whisper.

There was silence.

Then, 'Tell me that last statement doesn't mean what I think it means, Abby. Because I can't believe in this day and age that a man could do something like that without his wife's knowledge.'

Panic made her voice shriller than usual. 'I didn't know! I didn't! This house was in Orlando's name—'

Nick said something beneath his breath.

'We felt that it would be fairer that way—'

Dark brows were raised quizzically. '*We* felt?'

'Orlando felt,' admitted Abigail miserably, 'that it would make the relationship work better if he had something of his own. Anyway—' she shot him a militant look '—I knew about the flat. And the shares. And I know what he needed the money for.'

'You do?'

'Yes, I do! He was starting his own theatre company!' she retorted. 'He had bought the site and everything. I knew all that!'

'Like hell he had!' He levered himself out of the chair and hurled a log on the fire, which spat back at him like an angry cat. He gave her a piercing green stare. 'Just how well did you know your husband?'

She swallowed down the lump of fear which that piercing look provoked. 'As well as any wife,' she gulped, lying through her teeth.

'Really?' He raised his dark brows. 'Not well enough, in this case, it seems,' he remarked. 'Both the London and the New York money markets appear to have had a greater knowledge of your husband than you, Abby.'

'What are you trying to tell me?'

'That Orlando—as well as being a lousy actor and a compulsive liar—was an inveterate gambler.' He saw her disbelieving expression. 'Oh, you can shrug your pretty shoulders, if you like. I'm not talking about buying a few lottery tickets, or the occasional flutter on a horse. I'm talking big-time gambling here.' His face was suddenly sombre. 'And big-time debts, too. Believe me, Abby, when I tell you that the men Orlando owed money to are not the kind of men who take kindly to having to wait for their money, or to being short-changed.'

She stared at him in silence, the horror of what he was telling her dawning with each word he spoke.

'*Yes!*' he affirmed. 'Everything I'm telling you is true. And if I were you I'd take a good look at your portfolio, just to see how far he deceived you! To see just how effectively he has whittled away at your inheritance to pay off his debts.'

Her face was ashen, her mouth forming an incredulous question. 'I d-don't believe you,' she croaked.

'Believe me,' he responded implacably, and the emotionless Nick Harrington had, it seemed, returned with a vengeance. 'Contact your bank tomorrow and ask *them*, if you don't believe *me*. Try and find enough money to pay the bills and then see if you believe me!'

Abigail felt as though she were walking a tightrope—one false move and it would all be over. But there had to be a light at the end of this dark tunnel— there *had* to be. 'Even if what you say is true,' she said carefully clutching at straws, 'you forget, I still have all my mother's jewellery. It's worth a fortune. I can sell that.'

'Can you?' he challenged softly.

'Yes, I damn well can!'

'Hadn't you better make sure?' he suggested cruelly.

'Oh, I hate you, Nick Harrington!' she raged. 'You're simply revelling in every minute of this, aren't you?'

She didn't wait for his reply. Instead she ran from the room as if the hounds of hell were snapping at her heels, and back up the stairs—only this time to the bedroom she had once shared briefly with Orlando.

She had not set foot in the room for almost a year. An air of neglect had dulled the once beautiful bedchamber. The atmosphere was so stale and musty from lack of use that she half expected the rich hangings which surrounded the bed to be shrouded in cobwebs, like a scene from Dickens' *Great Expectations*.

Abigail shivered as she crouched down to open up the wall safe, and with hands which were icy cold she falteringly clicked in the combination.

The door flew open with a rewarding little snap, and Abigail stared inside, not believing the evidence of her eyes.

With a small cry, she began to scrabble around— the metal iron-cold against her chilled fingers—as though she could somehow magic up the sandalwood box containing the diamond rings and the exquisite sapphire set which Philip had given her mother on their wedding day. And all the other countless, glittering, costly trophies with which her mother had loved to adorn herself.

Gone, all gone.

The pig must have sold the lot!

Rightly or wrongly, she had always relied totally on her remarkable wealth—she had never known any other way. Money was her rock, the foundation on which her life had been built. Now it felt as though someone had whipped the carpet from beneath her feet, and she did not know whether she would have the strength to stand on her own.

As the reality washed over her, her knees buckled, and with a disbelieving shudder she sank to the floor, her eyes misting over as she began to say, over and over again, in a frantic plea, 'No, no, *no*! Oh, please,' she whispered. '*Someone*—please, tell me no!'

'No one can do that,' came an unforgiving voice from the door, and Abigail shuddered again as she looked up to see Nick standing there, so tall and dark, powerfully silhouetted against the light flooding in from the open door. 'It's gone, Abigail,' he emphasised softly. 'Every last bit of it. All gone. There's nothing left. Not a single thing.'

'You're enjoying this, aren't you?' she whispered.

His eyes gave nothing away. 'That, surely, is beside the point?'

She would not have him remembering her as a useless, crumbling wimp. She stood up to face him, pressing her lips together in a show of defiant pride. 'Well, I don't care!' she declared wildly. 'I'll come through this somehow!'

A reluctant touch of admiration tugged at the corners of his mouth. 'That's the spirit, Abby,' he applauded, with a murmur of approval. 'Glad to see that you've decided to model yourself on Scarlett O'Hara. No doubt by tomorrow morning you'll have ripped the curtains down and run yourself up a few dresses!'

She could have almost laughed at his outrageous sense of humour at a time like this, if the situation had not been so dire. 'Are you trying to be funny?'

'Not a good time, I agree.' He looked suitably chastened, fixing her with a melting look which could have started a thaw in Siberia. But Abigail resolutely set her heart against it.

'So what will you do?' he asked.

What indeed? She hunted around for inspiration. She thought of Mr Chambers, her bank manager, with his sober suit and his neat gold fountain-pen, and his pale earnest eyes gleaming from behind his round little spectacles. 'I'll go to the bank!' she pronounced. 'The manager has always had a soft spot for me; I should be able to get round him easily enough!'

The smile on Nick's mouth was wiped off and replaced by a withering look of contempt. 'Oh, should you?' he queried menacingly. 'And how will you do that, Abby? Flutter those lovely long eyelashes at him? Purse those soft lips into a little rosebud of a mouth? Or does your idea of persuasion have a rather more intimate slant to it? Will you let him unbutton your shirt, as you let me? Perhaps even part those milky white thighs for him...'

She stepped forward to slap his face, and this time he made no attempt to stop her. There was a loud, resounding crack as her hand connected with his cheek, but he didn't even flinch. In fact, if Abigail hadn't known how much he disliked her, she could have sworn that there was a fleeting look of something very like admiration in his eyes.

'Don't you ever dare speak to me like that again, Nick Harrington,' she told him with icy dignity. 'Or, believe me, I'll sue you for slander. Do you understand?'

'Was the accusation so way off the mark, then?'

'You know damned well it was! Or are you really suggesting that I would prostitute myself to my bank manager to get him to advance me some funds?'

'I guess not.' He shot her a rueful glance. 'I shouldn't have said it. I'm sorry.'

An admission of guilt! That, more than anything, calmed her down. She stared at him with frank amazement. 'Do you know, that's the first time you've ever said sorry to me?'

'Maybe it's the first time an apology has ever been warranted,' he suggested. 'But, just out of interest, are you serious? Do you really think that you can get any kind of loan with no collateral? They're going to make you sell this house, Abby,' he added urgently. 'They're going to have to. It's a bank—not a charity we're talking about.'

She had not believed him about the jewellery, but, with a sinking heart, she believed him now. Had he simply guessed the extent of Orlando's treachery, she wondered, or had he known?

'If you knew all this,' she said bitterly, 'then why didn't you warn me?'

'The New York apartment came on the market just

over a month ago,' he told her sombrely. 'It was only then that I started to investigate Orlando's affairs.'

She raised her chin in an accusatory stare, without thinking. 'And what about before that?' she demanded. 'Didn't it occur to you to—?'

'Check up on him?' he finished for her incredulously, and dumbly she nodded.

'Like a modern-day guardian angel, you mean?' He gave a cold, cynical laugh. 'Sorry, Abby, but marriage isn't a game, you know. When you plighted your troth, you took Orlando for richer and for *poorer*.'

She lifted her foot and aimed a vicious kick at one of the carved oak posts of the bed, symbol of her ruin and humiliation, then she turned back to him, her navy eyes almost black with distress. The seeming hopelessness of her situation yawned before her like an endless black tunnel. 'Then what am I going to do, Nick?' she asked him on a broken whisper. 'Just what am I to do?'

His eyes glittered with an emotion she found it impossible to define. 'You turn to me, Abby,' he said. 'And I will help you.'

CHAPTER FIVE

ABIGAIL stared at Nick as both hope and suspicion lit up her dark blue eyes so that they glittered like sapphires in her white face.

'You would help me?' she whispered. 'Really?'

He gave her a long, hard look. 'Of course I would help you. Did you think I would desert you and leave you to face potential ruin on your own?'

She shook her head, lost for words for once.

'What do you think brought me here today?' he demanded. 'Because it certainly wasn't a mark of respect for a man who almost succeeded in ruining you.'

What happened next was a knee-jerk reaction. It must have been. She blamed shock—the sham of her marriage, Orlando's tragic death, his double-dealing and deceit. That must have been what made her stand on tiptoe and fling her arms around Nick's neck, and cling onto him tightly, as if she couldn't bear to let him go.

'Oh, thank you, Nick!' she uttered fervently against his shoulder. 'Thank you! Maybe you aren't the cold, unfeeling brute I always thought you were! Maybe I've underestimated you for all these years!'

He had instinctively stiffened when she first hurled herself against him, but almost immediately he let his large, lean body relax, his hands roving to lie flatly over her hips, but the contact wasn't in the least bit sexual.

It was an embrace which made her feel safe and cosseted, and it was a million light years away from the way he had been holding her upstairs, on the bed. It could almost have been described as a hug, and hugs had been in pretty short supply in Abigail's life.

'Maybe you have,' he murmured with amusement, bending his head so that his mouth was on the silky curtain of her hair. 'Sorely underestimated me. And if this is your way of thanking me, Abby, then I have to tell you that I thoroughly approve.'

As usual he had spoilt it!

He probably thought he had all the right in the world to make remarks like that to her, after what she had let him do to her on her bed.

But perhaps she only had herself to blame. Because if she had not responded to him with such instant eagerness, then he might now be treating her with a little respect, instead of looking at her with that decidedly hungry expression in his eyes.

Yet, in spite of knowing that, and despising his attitude towards her, she still had to force herself to release herself from his grip. It felt too good to be pressed this close to him, to have those strong, capable hands cradling her hips in that innocent and yet possessive way. And, in so doing, he was somehow managing to make her feel more of a woman than she had ever felt before.

'Do you *always* have sex on the mind?' she demanded, moving away from him and tugging the grey sweater away from her chest, in a vain attempt to stop it from gluing itself to a pair of painfully erect nipples.

'Not on the mind, no,' he laughed, a wicked glint in the devilish green eyes. 'That isn't the customary part of the anatomy I use!'

'That wasn't what I meant, and you know it!'

'Abby, Abby, Abby,' he cajoled softly, with all the honeyed expertise of a snake-charmer, and Abigail had to steel herself not to succumb. 'One minute you're so delightfully responsive—and the next you're back to your old, combative self. And me being so benevolent, too.'

He *was* being benevolent. In fact, his entire demeanour seemed to have undergone a dramatic change once she had agreed to accept his offer of help. She narrowed her eyes suspiciously. 'Are you trying to blackmail me into going to bed with you?'

'Are you *serious*?'

She shrugged. 'Why not?'

He frowned. 'What kind of men have you been dealing with, for heaven's sake?' Then he nodded. 'Yes, of course. Silly of me. You had Orlando as a role model. Pretty unfortunate choice.' To her surprise he leaned forward and gently tilted her chin.

'Let's get one thing straight, right from the start, shall we? However your financial situation resolves itself—whatever help I give you—sex does not come into it. Or rather, if it does then it's unconnected.'

Abigail listened, almost hypnotised by the slumberous, sensual note in his voice, and a ripple of excitement tingled electric fingers over her breasts. 'I—I'm not entirely sure that I understand,' she managed. 'What it is you're saying?'

His eyes took on a smoky hue. 'I won't play games by denying that I want you, Abby, or that you want me—'

'Don't—'

'There's no need to blush,' he said smiling. 'There's nothing wrong with that. And obviously the natural conclusion to that desire is sex—and there's nothing wrong with that either, if it's what we both want to do. But it has to be a choice, Abby, and not a condition of my helping you.'

She found his words deeply disturbing, on a level she dared not analyse, but even worse was the calm, matter-of-fact, way he spoke about it. 'Do you have to put it quite so...so...' She struggled to find the right words.

'Mmm?'

'You make it sound...so...so—' She halted, unable to go on, her cheeks were burning so much.

'So *what*, Abigail?' he prompted wickedly, but his eyes were narrowed as he carefully observed her reaction.

'So mechanical!' she glared.

'Well, it *is* mechanical,' he mused. 'To a certain extent. It can also be highly emotional. Some say— and the poets would certainly have us believe it—that it can also reach an almost spiritual level.'

She heard the scepticism which coloured his voice. 'But not in your experience?'

'No,' he returned shortly. 'And in yours?'

She glowered at him indignantly. 'How the hell did we get onto this subject?'

He smiled. '*You* brought it up, as I recall. But I agree—it's time to change it. Talking about sex always gives me an appetite...'

She flashed him a warning glance, and yet in a way she felt liberated. He made it all sound so *normal*, so natural—not the way she was accustomed to thinking about sex at all.

'What food do you have in the house?' he queried innocently.

Food was the last thing on her overworked mind. 'I'm not sure. There are probably some sandwiches left—'

He grimaced. 'I need food, not dainty little nibbles. Let's go and see what we can find.'

The kitchen was not really Abigail's domain. During her marriage they had employed a series of cook-cum-housekeepers, who had usually been unable to tolerate Orlando's exacting standards for more than a couple of months. The last one had handed in her notice a few weeks ago, and left just before Orlando's death, and in the confusion of the following days Abigail hadn't got round to thinking about a replacement.

Still, he was right—they had to eat. She followed him out of the room and along the long, dark corridor to the kitchen.

Once there, Nick began searching through the large old-fashioned pantry with the experienced eye of a man used to fending for himself. 'There are eggs here,' he announced triumphantly, 'and pasta. See if there's any cheese and bacon in the fridge, will you, Abby?'

She opened the door of the fridge as gingerly as a spaceman entering an alien spaceship. 'There's cheese, but no bacon.'

'How about ham?'

Abigail peered inside. 'Lots of ham.'

'Good!' He straightened up. 'So I guess it all comes down to which of us makes the best carbonara.'

Abigail looked at him blankly. 'Sorry?'

'It's pasta, with egg and bacon—'

'I know what it *is*, Nick—I just can't cook it.'

He frowned slightly. 'Rubbish! anyone can cook pasta.'

She remembered her last attempt at a 'simple bolognese' and shook her head firmly. 'Not me.'

'Okay.' He shrugged. 'You can make the tea while *I* cook the pasta. And, of course, you get to load the dishwasher afterwards.'

'Lucky old me,' she said drily, thinking that he was very good at dishing out orders!

'I agree,' he murmured. 'Most women would move heaven and earth for a meal cooked by me!'

'Don't flatter yourself!'

Laughter lurked in the green eyes. 'I'm not!'

He certainly seemed very capable in the kitchen. And he was making her feel totally inadequate, decided Abigail as she hunted around for Earl Grey teabags, trying not to make it look as though she was on unfamiliar territory.

She was glad enough to have something to do with her hands, and something else to think about other than what a magnificent specimen Nick Harrington was—particularly when he was unaware that he was being watched.

Complaining that the kitchen was too hot, he had stripped off his forest-green sweater prior to chopping up what looked like a whole handful of garlic cloves. Underneath the sweater he wore a loose cambric shirt, but he immediately rolled up the sleeves to reveal two hair-roughened and brown muscular forearms. And if that wasn't enough he had undone the top two buttons of the shirt, revealing a tantalising glimpse of an equally hair-roughened chest.

Abigail sucked in a deep breath and had to force herself to tear her eyes away from him. There was no doubt about it—he was a spectacularly good-looking man.

Had she ever been so acutely aware of Orlando? she wondered. Had she ever just wanted to sit and dreamily watch *him*, appreciating the smooth, strong movement of *his* arms so enticingly hinted at beneath the fine linen shirts he'd worn?

She couldn't ever remember feeling that way about Orlando, she really couldn't—even in the beginning. And she doubted that he would have ever been so relaxed and so unselfconscious in her presence—indeed, in anyone's presence.

Whatever Orlando had done, he'd done for an audience—real or imagined. His stomach had always been tightly sucked in, his mouth always set in a soft, appealing pout. He'd known the position of every mirror in the house, and schooled his expression to greet them accordingly. If he'd moved with grace, it had been with the contrived grace he'd learnt at drama school. He had been, she realised sadly, the type of man who always looked over your shoulder at a party…looking for far more interesting fish to fry.

Nick glanced up from the steaming pan of spaghetti. 'Have you made the tea yet?'

'I've put two teabags in the mugs,' she told him helpfully.

He winced as he saw the results of her handiwork. 'Abby,' he said patiently, 'this is the kind of house that will not only have a magnificent silver teapot, but also the finest bone-china cups. We do not have to drink from those thick pottery mugs.'

'I happen to like them!'

'So do I. But not for tea. Tell you what,' he suggested, 'why don't I open a decent bottle of wine instead?'

A glass of wine might help her relax. Might stop her eyes following him so hypnotically, because sooner or later he was bound to notice. 'Good idea,' said Abigail, adding darkly, 'Unless Orlando has sold the lot!'

'Flogging wine is too much like hard work.'

Nick disappeared and returned minutes later with a bottle of Burgundy. He certainly seemed to have found his way round the place pretty quickly, thought

Abigail, as she went to the cupboard and selected two long-stemmed glasses. Though maybe it was just because he was that kind of man. Resourceful and decisive.

And, speaking of decisive—they still hadn't actually discussed what form his help was going to take. She shot him a covert look from beneath her dark lashes. Better wait until he'd eaten and drunk some wine. The more convivial his mood, the better.

And he might be a good cook, but he was also very bossy, she decided. He had Abigail fetching him pots and pans, laying the table and grating a large block of cheese into a bowl.

'Anything else you'd like me to do?' she asked sarcastically.

'Please. I found some Italian bread in the freezer—would you mind defrosting it?'

Abigail nervously put the glasses on the table and pretended not to hear him.

'Abby?'

She busied herself trying to fold a yellow napkin into a lily shape, but it ended up looking more like a scrambled egg.

'I'm about to serve up, so will you defrost the bread?'

Not unless he wanted incinerated ciabatta. 'I'm afraid I can't.'

'Can't?'

She met his curious gaze with a slightly shamefaced expression. 'I don't know how to use the microwave,' she confessed. 'Technology terrifies me.'

He digested this piece of information in silence, then he picked the loaf up, played a quick concertina on the array of buttons which adorned the front of the high-tech piece of equipment, and said, in a curiously bland voice, 'You'd better sit down, then.'

She watched him serving out the plates of pasta and felt annoyingly redundant, but even worse were the obvious waves of disapproval which were emanating from him, and which made her feel decidedly uncomfortable.

'It isn't my fault—' she began as she flicked an imaginary speck of dust from the pepper-mill.

'What isn't?'

'That I can't use the microwave...'

He slammed a fragrant plate down in front of her, before putting down his own and drawing up a chair opposite. 'No?' he queried repressively. 'Then whose fault is it, for God's sake? Orlando's? I'm afraid that my sympathy wears a little thin when you come out with outrageous statements like that, Abby!'

She slammed her fork down. 'I don't have to sit here and listen to you insult me!'

'No? Well, perhaps it's about time *someone* did, sweetheart! Maybe Orlando *did* rip you off, and maybe your trust in him *was* misplaced. That's unfortunate, yes. But what were you doing all the time he was going off and gambling your fortune away? You sure as hell weren't running a home for him to come back to!'

'Don't tell me that a liberated man of the nineties

subscribes to the idea that a woman should be *running a home*?' she demanded sarcastically.

He wound some pasta round his fork, Italian-style. 'If she doesn't happen to be working, then, yes,' he said deliberately.

'We had a housekeeper!' she defended, and then, seeing the look on his face, added, 'We *always* had a housekeeper!'

'So what?' he challenged. 'I have people working for me in my home, but I pride myself on being able to find my way around the kitchen without needing a map!'

'That isn't fair!' she howled.

'It damn well is!' There was silence while he poured two glasses of wine and then took an appreciative sip from his own. He shook his head in disbelief. 'Fancy not being able to use a microwave!'

'*Loads* of people can't use microwaves!'

'But not if they happen to *own* one!' He tore a piece of warm bread in half and took a thoughtful bite. 'How on earth did you manage on the housekeeper's day off?'

Might as well be hung for a sheep as a lamb. 'We ordered take-aways,' she admitted.

There was a shocked silence, and then he began to laugh. 'Oh, Abby,' he said eventually. 'You are priceless.'

She sipped her wine and heaved a surreptitious sigh of relief. That was better. Nick laughing—rare as that might be—was far more approachable than Nick ranting and raving and being critical.

She ate some of the pasta, and then some more, discovering just how hungry she really was. She devoured most of her portion as if it were going out of fashion, and when she looked up it was to find him watching her with the oddest expression in those grass-green eyes. He was probably amazed by her greed, she thought, rather guiltily.

'This is delicious,' she said, rather lamely.

'Obviously.' His eyes glinted.

'I wouldn't usually eat so much,' she told him defensively.

He frowned. 'Then you should. I like to see a woman enjoying her food. It isn't a crime, Abby,' he finished softly.

To Orlando it had been a crime. He had watched her waistline like a hawk, obsessed by her outward appearance while managing not to be attracted to it at the same time.

'I'll teach you how to cook it, if you like,' Nick offered. 'I'm sure that even a technophobe like yourself could manage to turn the oven on!'

But his teasing offer only reminded her that no decisions had actually been made about her future. Abigail put her fork carefully down on the plate.

She supposed that this house *was* too big to keep up on her own, and, even if it wasn't, she definitely wanted to eradicate all associations with Orlando.

She paused while her brain sought for a diplomatic way to broach the subject without sounding greedy and grasping. 'Um, Nick?' She hesitated delicately.

His eyes narrowed. 'Abby?'

'It's terribly kind of you to offer to help me—'

'I think so, too,' he agreed equably.

'And I thought that perhaps it might be best to discuss it now. After all, I expect you'll be back off to wherever it is you're going tomorrow, won't you?'

He leaned back in his chair, sipping his wine and staring at her with amusement. 'So keen to get rid of me, are you?'

'Not at all,' she answered immediately, although she wasn't sure that she was being entirely truthful with him. It wasn't so much that she wanted him to go, just that she was rather worried about what might happen if he stayed!

'And will you miss me, Abby?' he mused. 'Honestly?'

She gulped. Was the man a mind-reader, or what? 'You can't expect me to answer that *honestly*, when you're just about to come to my rescue.'

'You make me sound like a knight on a white charger,' he mocked.

She stabbed her fork into a swirl of spaghetti which seemed to have a life of its own. 'Do I? I didn't mean to,' she told him truthfully.

He smiled at this. 'So, will you miss me?'

She hesitated.

'Remember what I said earlier,' he said wryly. 'There are no conditions to my helping you. You can shoot straight from the hip—I won't be offended.'

'Then I probably won't…miss you, that is.' Giving up on the spaghetti, she put her fork down and twirled the stem of her wineglass between her fingers, expecting him to look affronted.

But to her surprise he looked merely amused. 'And why's that?' he queried idly. 'Seriously, Abby. I'm interested. You have the dubious honour of having seen me in some of my formative years. So you know me very well—certainly more than any other woman—apart from my mother, of course.'

Abby's mouth softened automatically. 'How is your mother?'

He gave a wry smile. 'Fine. Stubborn. Nothing changes.'

'I get a long letter from her every Christmas, but that's it,' said Abby. 'She says she's too busy to write much.'

'She is,' he said darkly. 'And quite unnecessarily so, in my opinion.'

She heard the suppressed irritation in his voice. 'Oh? Why?'

'Well, this dutiful son finds that he wants to shower her with enough money and security to cushion her in her twilight years…'

She threw him a questioning look. 'But?'

'But she steadfastly refuses to accept it.'

'Why?'

'Because she still insists on cooking for a living,' he growled.

Lucky Rosita, thought Abigail fleetingly. To have the pride and the wherewithal to refuse her arrogant son. 'And what's wrong with that? Your mother cooks for a living. She's brilliant at it and she enjoys it. You surely don't want to stop her doing that?'

He threw her an ironic glance. 'I find it rather odd that you should be defending my mother's right to work—you, who have never done a day's honest toil in your life.'

She put her wineglass down and looked up at him seriously. 'Are you intending to make my situation even more intolerable by making comments like that all the time?'

He shook his dark head. 'Not at all. But we seem to have drifted from our original topic.' He raised his glass to her in a mocking kind of toast.

'Which was? Remind me, I've forgotten.'

'Just why you find me so unmissable?'

'You really want to know?'

He smiled. 'Really, really!'

'Okay, then.' She began to count on her fingers. 'Your arrogance. Your high-handedness. Your criticism. All of which were very effectively illustrated by our last conversation.' She looked at him quizzically. 'Shall I continue?'

He grimaced, then laughed. 'Spare me. And I used to have such a healthy ego!'

Abigail laughed, too, and it sounded strange to her ears—it seemed such a long time since she had laughed so unrestrainedly. A glimpse of normal, ordinary living—the kind that Orlando had always despised—leapt tantalisingly into her mind.

Just for a moment, sitting casually opposite Nick at the kitchen table, with the room all warm and bright and the remains of the scratch supper in front of them, she got a fleeting idea of what *real* companionship could be like.

Orlando would never have dreamed of sitting down to a simple meal like this, not in a million years. He had always been lured by the bright glitter of up-market restaurants, in which her money had allowed him to indulge.

And even when they *had* eaten here, in this magnificent house, it had always been a grand production in the formal, rather stuffy dining-room—with guests flown in and temporary staff taken on to indulge all their sybaritic whims.

She had enjoyed tonight, she realised, and following on from that thought came another, quickly in its wake. She had lied, because, yes, she *was* going to miss him.

Better by far that he was due to leave tomorrow, she told herself briskly. Already she had started weaving pathetic little fantasies about him. Much more of that spelt danger.

He was glancing around curiously at the spacious, high-ceilinged kitchen, and when he looked at her again he seemed perplexed. 'Just tell me one thing, Abby—what in the world did you *do* all day in this big house?'

What indeed? She stared into the ruby depths of her wineglass before slowly raising her head to meet his gaze. 'I used to go into London a lot…'

'What for?'

'Oh, you know, shopping…sometimes. Lunch. Galleries. The usual thing.'

'A lady-who-lunches?' he asked deliberately.

'You sound as though you don't approve?'

'That's because I don't!'

Abigail sighed. She couldn't face another bout of sparring, not today, and not with Nick. He always seemed to win. It was time to grab the bull by the horns. 'I think it's time to decide what we're going to do,' she said.

His face was shuttered. 'Go on.'

'You're the financial expert. I'd like you to come with me to see Mr Chambers, my bank manager, tomorrow. Obviously this house is much too big to keep on, and I certainly wouldn't expect *you* to pay for its upkeep.'

He put his glass down on the table. 'Oh, wouldn't you?' he queried steadily, his face poker-straight. 'Just what did you have in mind, then, Abby?'

'Well…' The words started to come out in a rush, she was so eager to get them over with. 'A small flat in London might be best, mightn't it?'

'Which I presume you're proposing that I buy for you?'

She hesitated. 'Well, yes.'

'I see.' His face had never looked more expressionless. 'And while you're living in this ''small flat'' just how do you intend supporting yourself?'

She opened her blue eyes very wide. 'I thought…' Lord alive, but he was making her squirm!

'Yes, Abby? What did you think?'

'I thought that you might give me an income—'
She saw something horribly disapproving on his face,
and so she hastily amended it. 'Just a tiny one, of
course.'

'I see.' There was a moment's silence before he
resumed, in a heavier voice than before. 'So, basically, Abby, all you want from me is just a ''small''
flat and a ''tiny'' income. Is that right?'

She frowned. 'There's no need to put it quite like
that—you make me sound positively mercenary.'

'Do I?' he enquired silkily. 'I'm only repeating
your own words to me. How else do you suggest that
I should put it?'

She impatiently scooped a rope of shining hair back
over her shoulder. 'You can afford it! You're fabulously rich—everyone knows that.'

'And *you* are fabulously spoilt, Abigail! Is this help
to take the form of a gift? Or a loan? And, if so, how
do you propose to repay me?'

She bit her bottom lip. 'I hadn't really thought that
far ahead.'

'Apparently not.' He fixed her with an unwavering
look.

'So you aren't going to help me?'

He smiled a seemingly bland smile, but there was
a distinctly dangerous quality to it which made
Abigail more uneasy than anything he had said before.
'I've said I'll help you, and I will. But it is not going
to take the form of dishing you up any more in the
way of hand-outs!'

'Hand-outs?' she declared indignantly.

'Yes, hand-outs!' He glowered at her. 'Ever since the day your mother married Philip you've had more lavished on you than is healthy—and consequently you've grown up into a poor little rich girl who thinks that the world owes her a living!'

Abigail half rose from her chair. 'I don't have to stay here and listen to this!'

His face was triumphant. 'Oh, but that's just where you're wrong, sweetheart, I'm afraid that you do! There's no one left for you to turn to but me. Is there? Maybe Orlando has done you a kind of favour after all. He's freed you from the burden of your inheritance. It's time to come out into the real world, Abigail—and start living!'

Something in his dark smug face made her want to shake him! 'You're loving all this, aren't you?' she demanded. 'Expecting me to crawl to you—to *beg* you for money! Well, I'm not going to! I would rather *starve* than beg you for anything, Nick Harrington!'

'I think I would rather enjoy seeing you begging,' he murmured cryptically. 'But even if you did I wouldn't give you anything.'

'So you lied! You lied! You *aren't* going to help me?'

He shook his dark head. 'Oh, but I am—I am. More than you'll ever know. And one day you'll thank me for it, Abigail.'

She blinked at him in confusion. 'I don't understand.'

'Then let me explain. You're going to *earn* your

keep, Abby, in the way that everyone else does. By *working* for it.'

'But working at *what*? she demanded. 'I can't actually *do* anything! Who on earth is going to employ someone like me?'

There was the glimmer of a sardonic smile. 'Why, me, of course. Who else?'

CHAPTER SIX

'I CAN'T believe that this is happening,' said Abigail stubbornly, and heard Nick give that low, mocking laugh which so infuriated her. In future she must remember not to complain so much about her predicament—it seemed to give him an inordinate amount of pleasure.

'A sense of unreality?' he murmured, his thigh tensing as he depressed the accelerator pedal and the car picked up speed. 'Then fix your eyes on the horizon, my dear. That's real enough.'

'That isn't what I meant and you know it,' she grumbled, but she lapsed into silence anyway and watched the landscape whizzing by, the trees and hedges and fields being replaced by ever more roads and houses as they got closer and closer to London.

In the two days since Orlando's funeral so much seemed to have happened. No. So much *had* happened. And Nick had been the instigator. He was the kind of man who, once he made a decision, could turn a woman's world upside down.

But it had been more than his decisiveness which had amazed her, for over the past forty-eight hours he had revealed sides to his character that she would never have dreamed existed.

She did not know what she had been expecting

from him, but it had certainly not been the kindness and the understanding he had demonstrated that first night after the funeral, when she had been so reluctant to go to bed and yet unwilling to tell him why.

For once he had not hounded her with questions, but had let her sit in silence, drinking a huge glass of brandy in front of the roaring fire to which he kept adding more and more logs as the evening wore on.

Nick had been sitting on the big sofa opposite, reading the kind of book which won prizes and which most people read because they felt they *ought* to—but he had actually seemed to be *enjoying* it!

Abigail had done nothing but stare into the dancing flames, an immense sadness for Orlando's death eating away inside her which she did not feel ready to share with anyone.

Not even Nick.

When she had begun to yawn he had disappeared and returned with a large cup of herbal tea which he'd insisted she drink with lots of honey added. After that she'd been almost unable to keep her eyes open, and he had told her, quite severely, that it was time she was in bed.

So masterful, she'd thought, rather sinfully. In her half-asleep, highly emotional state, she had fleetingly wondered whether he intended going the whole hog by carrying her upstairs to bed, and she had been more than a little bit disappointed when he'd merely walked beside her up the huge staircase.

She'd found that he had lit a fire in her bedroom, and had added apple-wood and pinecones to the now smouldering coals, so that the air was warm and sweet and heavy, and her eyes had closed just as soon as she'd put the light out and said a muffled goodnight to him.

It was the first time she had slept without being haunted by bad dreams since her wedding night...

And the following morning, instead of going to the bank to see Mr Chambers, Nick had insisted that Mr Chambers come to the house, and, to Abigail's surprise, the bank manager had obediently complied, trotting up the steps to the house like an obedient dog.

Once he'd arrived, Nick had taken over completely, clearing space around the huge round dining-table. And there the three of them had sat, Nick with his shirtsleeves rolled up again—wearing a gorgeous pale chartreuse-coloured shirt which had made his eyes look the colour of a lush green glade.

After her surprisingly good night's sleep, and having demolished two slices of toast and marmalade for breakfast, Abigail had felt more alive than she had done in years.

It had, perhaps, been unfortunate that her new vitality should have manifested itself in an inability to be in the same room as Nick without being acutely aware of just what a devastating man he was.

Or perhaps she had always known, and had just blocked out the thoughts because they were futile and unwelcome?

Or had it just happened because he had kissed her? Awoken her senses with the magic of his touch, like in all the best fairy stories?

She had thought that Orlando—with his cruel taunts and lack of finesse—had killed off every last vestige of sexual desire in her, so it was something of a shock to find that this was not so.

Not at all.

Quite the opposite, in fact.

And, even though maths had been her very worst subject at school, it had been relief of a kind when Mr Chambers had arrived and she'd been able to concentrate on something other than how Nick could make even the simplest act—like pulling back the velvet curtains to let the winter sunshine stream in—the most transfixingly sensual movement imaginable.

Abigail had been mystified by the figures which Nick and Mr Chambers had discussed so fluently, and had tried to leave the room on the pretext of making them all some coffee.

That was when Nick had told her that she made the worst coffee in the world, and that *he* would make the coffee while she studied all the different graphs he had drawn for her.

He must have worked hard on them the night before, after he had sent her up to bed. They'd been very clear and very simple graphs, but all the different figures had made her head spin, and, when she'd asked Nick to tell her in words of one syllable what they all actually meant, he had replied, in a rather dark and sombre voice, 'The bottom line is that you're broke, Abby. Flat broke. Even when the house is sold.'

She waited until Mr Chambers drove off in his sensible family saloon before she dared ask Nick the fairly obvious question which should have occurred to her the night before. 'How on earth do you expect me to work for a man like you when I can't, um…actually *do* anything?'

He gave her a brief, crinkly smile before replying. 'Your state of blissful ignorance will last only until we reach London—then you'll be taught a whole lot of new skills which will equip you for life. And which you should have learned years ago,' he concluded darkly.

'What kind of skills?'

'I'll leave you to work that out for yourself.'

She didn't dare try! 'And who's going to teach me?' she squeaked.

'You'll just have to wait and see,' he evaded.

And no power that she possessed could persuade him to elaborate any further. 'I'd forgotten just how stubborn you could be,' she told him.

'Guilty as charged,' he agreed.

And yet he complained about that self-same stubbornness in his own mother!

'That's my final offer, Abby,' he told her airily. 'You can take it or leave it.'

Which left Abigail with no alternative but to accept. And she might have accepted it with grace if he hadn't been so blatantly triumphant. As it was, she muttered a rather tight 'thank you', from between gritted teeth, suspecting that Nick Harrington was going to take very great pleasure in bossing her around!

And now they were zooming into London over the

Hammersmith flyover, with Nick's bright red sports car drawing admiringly jealous glances from other road-users.

He roared past a Porsche.

'You aren't a formula-one driver on the side, are you?' she enquired waspishly.

'Why? Does my driving bother you?'

'Oh, you're *driving*, are you? I thought you were trying to break the world speed-record!'

'I'm actually just within the limit. Why? Does it frighten you?'

She found it rather thrilling, actually, though the last thing she would do was admit it! 'Marginally less than the thought of sharing a kitchen with you!'

He laughed. 'I can see that living with you is going to be stimulating in more ways than one.'

She shot him a sideways glance. 'Meaning?'

'Meaning that I like a woman who gives as good as she gets!' And he put his foot down on the accelerator, sending them screeching up the road.

Abigail tried not to enjoy the speed and his expert driving. Why did a half-baked compliment like that set her heart hammering so loud that she was certain his quadraphonic sound-system must be transmitting it?

What on earth was happening to her?

Was it just Nick and the way he had blazed into her life and transformed it? Was that why she felt as though she had shaken off the dull blanket which had shrouded her during her marriage and started to emerge as a person? A real person, who was getting more real by the minute?

'Do you think that the two of us sharing a flat is a good idea?' she ventured, knowing that she would die if he said no.

'No.'

'Oh.'

'You shouldn't ask the question if you can't stand to hear the answer! First rule of life!' He shot her an amused side-glance. 'But there's no need to look so crestfallen, Abby...'

'I am *not* crestfallen,' she said, with as much dignity as she could muster. 'You happen to be echoing my own sentiments entirely!' Then her air of icy reserve crumbled as curiosity sliced through it. '*Why* don't you think that—?'

'Our sharing a flat is a good idea?' His mouth quirked as he smoothly changed down a gear. 'Do you really need to ask me that?'

Had she succeeded in embarrassing *him* for a change? 'Yes,' she said sweetly. 'I do.'

'I should say that the overwhelming sexual attraction between us would be the most obvious obstacle,' he commented drily.

Abigail's hands leapt to her burning cheeks. How could he *say* something like that? So openly? So brazenly? But what disappointed her more than anything was the almost clinical way in which he spoke of sexual attraction, without any mention of the feelings which that attraction might inspire.

Were all men, then, the same in their outlook on such matters?

'So why not find me somewhere else to live?' she challenged.

'Oh, I've considered it,' he admitted. 'Long and hard. And, on balance, I decided that you would be more safe with me than without me.'

'Why?'

He shrugged and smiled when a redhead flashed him a provocative grin as she overtook him in a similarly zippy little sports car and then roared off in a cloud of exhaust fumes. 'That was a very foolish piece of driving,' he observed slowly. 'Very foolish indeed.'

'If you could just drag your eyes away from that driver for a moment,' said Abigail crossly, 'and answer my question! Why am I safer with you than somewhere else?'

He clicked off the stereo so that the music stopped abruptly, filling the car with silence. 'Because you are essentially an innocent,' he said.

Abby held her breath, her heart thudding madly as she wondered what was coming next...

'Basically, you've been protected from the real world all your life—those crazy schools and then that equally crazy marriage. It isn't just your fault—'

'Thanks,' she said sarcastically.

'But even if I arranged a room in a girlfriend's flat—well, you'd be bound to meet men...'

'And that isn't allowed?'

He shot her a narrow-eyed glance. 'Not at the moment, no. I think it's inadvisable. I think you need to lick your wounds. To have a little space to recover. To find yourself, as they say in all the best counselling sessions.'

'Don't tell me that *you've* had counselling sessions?' Abigail exclaimed in surprise.

He gave a lazy smile. 'What do you think?'

She thought that he hadn't. He seemed so strong, so resolute, so in control. Although she had, come to think of it, seen a glimpse of him losing his cool in the last two days. It would be interesting to know whether that formidable self-restraint could ever be shattered completely.

He carefully avoided a cyclist who seemed to have a death wish. 'Oh, don't misunderstand me,' he elaborated, after a moment's thought. 'I think that the current trend for exploring feelings works very well for some people.'

'But not for you?'

'No,' he agreed shortly. 'Not for me.'

Was he one of those men who considered it weak to acknowledge their own feelings? wondered Abigail. Were men really so different from women in that respect?

She stared out of the window, uncomfortable suddenly, and with a rather urgent desire to change the subject. 'Tell me about the flat.'

'It isn't a flat—it's a house.' He glanced in his rearview mirror. 'We'll be there soon, so you can see for yourself. It's in Kensington, it's very pretty, and you can walk to the park in minutes.'

'How long have you lived there?'

'Not long enough. Whenever I'm based in London. But I move around, as you know. My work takes me to all the major cities, and the headquarters of my company are now in New York.'

Abigail knew very little about Nick's other life. Her stepfather had described Nick as a 'wheeler-dealer'—whatever that meant. 'What kind of business is it, exactly? I've never really understood.' She eyed the plush leather interior of the car. 'Apart from being an obviously lucrative one?'

'I'm a troubleshooter.' He gave a small smile and changed gear smoothly as a lorry tried to cut them up. 'If a business is doing badly—I mean *really* badly—then they call me in.'

'And what's that? The kiss of death?'

He laughed. 'I don't work on every case myself; I have a team of experts working for me. But when I do, I look very closely at the way the company has been operating. I take it apart—nuts and bolts—and try to find out where they've been going wrong.'

'And is that easy?'

'Never,' he admitted quietly. 'I'm their last-ditch attempt—they've usually tried just about everything else. It's especially difficult if it's an old, established family firm which, for whatever reason, has failed to keep up with technological advances.' He shot her a frowning look, and Abigail was reminded of her lack of skill with the microwave!

'They are the ones I try really hard to put back on their feet,' he said.

'Careful, Nick,' she warned. 'That sounded like a touch of sentimentality creeping in.'

'I know—worrying, isn't it?'

They drove for a while in a silence which could have almost been called companionable.

'But I'd like to know where *I'm* supposed to fit in with all this,' said Abby, after a while. 'Someone who can't type, can't work a switchboard, can't work a microwave and—'

'Can't stop talking for a moment,' he interrupted, his attention elsewhere as the car slid to a halt by a zebra crossing.

A blonde, in a thigh-skimming leather mini-skirt with matching bomber jacket, was walking a white poodle across the black and white stripes. She did a double take when she saw Nick behind the wheel and took for ever to clip-clop the short distance, swaying her hips like a limbo dancer.

Abigail turned to see Nick smiling appreciatively as he revved up the car again. 'Perhaps you'd like to stop and offer her a lift?' she asked.

He shrugged. 'Unfortunately, it's only a two-seater. Anyway—not my type.'

'Oh?' She could hardly prevent herself from smiling.

'No. Can't stand poodles.'

Nick's house was in a proper, old-fashioned London square, with iron railings fencing off the beautifully maintained area of grass in the middle. There were wooden benches to sit on beneath mature trees, which Abigail could see would provide a beautiful green canopy when they were in leaf.

'Like it?' he asked.

'Mmm! It's the kind of house Mary Poppins lived in!' she said dreamily, and he smiled.

'All the house-owners have a key to unlock the gate to the garden,' he explained as he opened the door of the car for her. 'It's a bit like the secret garden. In the springtime hundreds and hundreds of bulbs come out—daffodils and snowdrops and tiny blue irises. It attracts all kinds of birds, kinds you would never expect to see in central London, although, of course, some of them fly over from the park.'

'It's beautiful,' enthused Abigail, managing somehow to mask her surprise. What with the car and the image—the jet-setting, glamorous lifestyle—she hadn't really imagined Nick to be the type to rave over flowers and notice the birds!

There were steps up to the front door, which was painted a glossy delphinium-blue, and he put her suitcases down and unlocked it.

'I'll give you a guided tour, shall I?' he said as she followed him into the hall.

'Thanks,' she replied, rather faintly. She didn't know what kind of place she had imagined he might live in, but it was certainly not this. He had been such a dab hand with the microwave that she had thought he might have one of those open-plan modern flats, with a wall of glass overlooking the river and streamlined uncomfortable furniture.

But this was elegant and restrained, with high ceilings and crafted mouldings and bright rooms which were astonishingly quiet. Who would ever imagine that the busy London streets were merely a stone's throw away?

'The kitchen is in the basement. So is the dining-room, and that overlooks the garden. The large room which takes up most of the ground floor I use as an office, but it's decorative as well as functional. The sitting-room is on the next floor, with a bathroom, too, and then the bedrooms are above that. The stairs will keep you fit,' he observed with a glint of humour as they reached the top of the house.

'Don't I look fit, then?' she queried immediately.

'Don't fish for compliments,' he offered drily, and flung open one of the bedroom doors. 'This is yours.'

It was a big, airy room, with a vast window overlooking the bare splendour of a winter garden where a small grey fountain bubbled mysteriously beneath a cypress tree. The walls were covered in delicate watercolours and the bed had an exquisitely embroidered throw covering it, but Abigail scarcely noticed her surroundings, for her attention was caught by the small, rough clay figure which stood in pride of place on the windowsill.

It was of a horse, a horse caught in mid-gallop with its nostrils flared and its muscles rippling. It was a crudely depicted little thing, and Abigail had not seen it for almost five years.

She had made it for Nick. For Christmas.

It had been a bit of a joke at the time. Abigail had loved horses, and yet had been petrified of them at the same time. Philip had promised her a horse of her own, but it had taken until she was fourteen for her to summon up the courage to have lessons at school, and then the reality of the huge, powerful creatures, snorting hot air and whinnying like mad, had put her off for life.

During the vacation Nick had teased her and teased her about it, and, just to show him that she didn't care, she had made him the figurine in her art class and given it to him for Christmas.

She picked it up with trembling fingers, trying to convince herself that it was just the sharp memory of childhood which was making her feel so tearful. And not the fact that she was unbearably touched by the fact that he had kept it.

But it was no good. She looked up at him with brimming eyes. 'Nick?' she whispered, and, to her utter astonishment, his face took on a haunted expression which she was certain reflected her own feelings exactly.

Surely that wasn't Nick Harrington looking all choked up, too? Abigail thought with amazement.

But the moment passed, and within seconds he had regained his customary aplomb, though his voice was inordinately gentle as he said quietly, 'Cry if you feel the need to, sweetheart, but that wasn't my intention when I put it there.'

She spoke in a wobbly voice, though more because of his gentleness than anything else. 'J-just why *did* you put it there?' she said, stumbling over the words.

His eyes were as soft and as rich as green velvet.

'I thought you might be feeling lost, and a little home-sick—that you might appreciate something from your past. It was something to welcome you, if you like.'

She opened her eyes very wide. 'Did you *plan* to bring me back here with you, Nick?'

He looked surprised that she had even thought otherwise. 'Of course I did.'

'And what if I'd said no?'

'You weren't in any position to say no, were you? And even if you had been,' he stated, rather ominously, 'I wasn't going to give you a chance. Not this time,' he added, and she knew from the hostile glitter in his eyes that he was referring to his opposition to her marriage.

She looked down at the statue, which, for all its imperfection, had been made with the uninhibited passion of youth.

She remembered Nick's face as he had opened up the parcel which contained it on Christmas morning— the swift, unguarded look of pleasure which had crossed his face as he had lifted the crude shape from the wrapping-paper.

He was a man who rarely let his feelings show— not even on Christmas Day, when he had always joined the family for lunch, a meal he'd helped his mother cook. That he had always done it under sufferance was now glaringly obvious to her.

Only now could Abigail recognise what a tussle it must have been for the ambitious young man to be cast in a servile role—no matter how kind Philip and her mother had been to him. Through no fault of his own, he had been the reluctant recipient of patronage, however well intended, and for a man with Nick's fierce, innate pride, that must have been difficult to take.

Over the years she had convinced herself that the relationship between herself and Nick had been one fundamentally blighted by distrust and dislike. Now she conceded that it had *not* been that black and white. That there had been good times, too.

He was looking at her curiously as her fingers slowly caressed the dappled clay of the horse. 'You looked miles away.'

'I was. Remembering when I gave this to you.'

'Christmas Day.' He pulled a face. 'We rowed later. Do you remember that?'

'Did we? Over what?'

The corners of his mouth threatened to lift in a smile. 'Over a skirt.'

And what a skirt, she recalled suddenly. And, come to think of it, Nick had lost control that time, too.

The fashion at the time had been for minis, but Abigail's had been simply an excuse for a skirt. Bought from the hottest shop in London, it had barely skimmed her bottom.

At fourteen, she had been full of insecurities about her looks, and had wanted to look her best for the pack of actors Philip had invited, and who were arriving for drinks before lunch.

She had ummed and ahhed for ages about the wisdom of wearing it, and had been glancing over her shoulder into one of the long mirrors in her bedroom, when a sudden reflected movement had caught her eye.

Walking out onto the balcony, Abigail had looked down into the brightness of the Californian sunshine to see Nick standing by the pool, with the sunlight burnishing his coal-dark hair.

He had stared up at her for a long moment in stunned disbelief, then disappeared. Moments later he had arrived unannounced at her door, his face black as thunder as his eyes skimmed over her skimpy outfit.

'What the *hell* do you think you're wearing?' he'd demanded.

It hadn't mattered that she had been in two minds whether or not to wear it. Or that his outraged tone had given her a surprisingly primitive little kick of pleasure. She hadn't liked his tone one bit. 'What does it look like?' she'd returned sweetly.

'Take it off!' he'd snarled.

Without thinking, she'd answered in the way that one of her more precocious classmates might have done, putting her hands on her pubescent hips, and purring, 'Why, Nick, is that a proposition?'

She knew now why she had pushed the memory to the farthest corner of her mind, for the look of absolute disgust on his face before he had slammed his way out of her room had haunted her for months afterwards…

She put the horse carefully back down on the window sill. 'I'm surprised you kept it all these years.'

His mouth twisted into a sardonic smile. 'Senti-mentality again, you mean?'

She thought about it. 'Yes, I suppose I do.'

'And does sentimentality shock you so much?'

'Yes,' she answered, frankly. 'If it's associated with you!'

'And my heart of stone?' he mocked.

Abigail met his candid stare, and shrugged. 'Well, you said it.'

'Maybe I was hoping for a contradiction?'

'Sorry to disappoint you.'

'Oh, but you didn't,' he responded softly, and ran his thumb slowly and thoughtfully along the strong curve of his jawline.

Just a little thing, but she followed the movement hungrily, her eyes drawn helplessly to the hint of blue-black shadow around his chin. It was such a strong face, she thought wistfully. Healthy and clean and strong. The kind of face you would want the fa-ther of your children to have...

As she watched him turn a coolly quizzical gaze in her direction she became acutely aware of his pow-erful physical presence, and was suddenly struck with a bizarre attack of nerves. Was he conscious of how badly he could affect her?

'So, here I am in Kensington,' she said hastily, moving away on the pretext of straightening one of the blue and yellow cushions which littered the large bed. 'Where do I go from here?'

He smiled, clearly at ease with his role of being in control, and Abigail discovered that you could resent someone's attitude and yet long for them to touch you all at the same time.

'You unpack your cases while I make us some coffee,' he said. 'And tomorrow you start college.'

It was a good thing she had put the horse down, for she certainly would have dropped it. *'College!'* she exclaimed. 'To do what?'

He sounded like a man who had been reading prospectuses. 'To learn office skills and to type. And to be literate in the three most commonly used computer packages,' he rattled off. 'It makes sense, Abby.'

He might as well have challenged her to become fluent in Russian and Chinese within the next twenty-four hours. Abigail's heavy-lidded blue eyes widened. 'You *are* kidding?'

'I am not.'

No. He wasn't. His face was entirely serious.

'It's just what you need,' he said. 'Basic skills which will make you instantly employable; how you build on them is up to you. And you don't *have* to work for me, afterwards, not really.'

'I—don't?' she queried, aware of an infuriating little tug of disappointment.

'Not if you think you're going to find me too much of an ogre. I use the very best secretarial agency whenever I'm in town. Sandie, the owner, happens to be a good friend of mine. If you work hard, I'm sure that she will employ you in some capacity. But first things first. Just do the course.'

In spite of her misgivings, Abigail actually began to feel excited.

'And just how long is this course going to take me?'

His smile was triumphant. 'It's going to take you precisely three weeks,' he said, in the most determined voice she had ever heard him use. 'It's the fastest in London.'

CHAPTER SEVEN

PITMAN'S COLLEGE was a peculiar old building, which had once been a hospital, and still housed the vast and ancient lifts which had been used to carry patients to the operating theatre to prove it. Outside, on the mellowed brick wall, hung an equally ancient and rather ugly clock, much loved by the staff and students alike.

It was situated in the heart of London, in Russell Square. There was a small park in the centre of the square, where the students tended to eat their sandwiches at lunchtime, weather permitting.

On Abigail's first morning Nick took her there in his car, but the bright red racy model always drew attention—and not always welcome attention, Abigail realised with a sudden flash of insight as she saw what were probably to be her fellow students struggling off the bus and coming from the tube.

'I'll come by myself tomorrow,' she told him firmly as she unclipped her seat belt, trying and failing not to be impressed with the way he looked.

He was dressed in an amazingly understated charcoal suit for work, whereas she was clad in a pair of faded jeans with matching jacket, which she had managed to unearth as being suitable for a student. His

125

hair was still dampish from the shower and she longed to straighten his tie for him.

'And how will you do that?' he drawled, as he retrieved a pencil she had dropped down by his foot and handed it to her.

'By bus. Or by tube, of course,' she told him. 'The way most people travel around London.'

'It's no problem to drive you—'

'I don't want to stand out, Nick,' she told him firmly. 'I want to fit in. It's important, if I'm to do well.'

He gave a slow smile. 'And I have a distinct feeling you are going to do well.'

Oh, yes. She had already decided that she would do *very* well. She had lain awake in bed the previous night, replete with the chicken casserole which Nick had shown her how to make, and had done a lot of thinking.

The oddest thing was that she *didn't* feel in the least bit hard done by, or the remotest bit sad that she had gone from being extremely wealthy to having nothing, comparatively speaking. It was, she had discovered, all a matter of attitude. She looked on it as an adventure—as a chance to start again and to make something of her life. And she had vowed that she would show Nick just how much she could achieve.

More importantly, she would show herself.

'If that's the way you want it,' he sighed, but he was still smiling.

'I do.'

Later, of course, standing at the bus-stop, lashed by

the rain and weighted down by her load of new text-books, Abigail could have kicked herself, thinking of the warm, plush leather interior of Nick's car and the smooth way it had of zipping round the capital.

But by the time she had arrived home to an empty house, showered and changed, then made herself a cup of tea, she felt a million times better, and settled herself at the kitchen table to practise on the keyboard of the electric typewriter which Nick had thoughtfully installed there for her.

Proficiency in typing was, she told herself with de-termination as she echoed the words of her course tutor, just a matter of practice. She spread her fingers out experimentally over the keyboard.

Nick arrived home an hour later to find her sitting with her eyes closed, punching out the practice rhymes over and over again, her honey-coloured hair newly washed and gleaming all the way down her back.

He smiled, noting the teapot which stood before her. 'Any left?' he queried, dropping a slim black leather briefcase on the floor.

'It will be cold. I'll make us another.' Abigail stood up with an air of calm authority, but felt stupidly aware of herself in the most self-conscious way imagi-nable. Did the faded jeans she wore hug her bottom too closely? she wondered. Or the long-sleeved corn-flower-blue body draw the eye to her breasts too much? And would Nick make some clever crack about the way she was busying herself around the place, warming the teapot?

Nick sat watching her in silence. If he *had* noticed her dramatic change of attitude where domesticity was concerned, then he was diplomatic enough not to say anything other than a rather laconic, 'Mmm. That'd be nice.' And then he'd sprawled with careless grace in a chair, following her movements with apparent fascination as she tried to familiarise herself with the new kitchen.

After that, her typing went to pot. It was impossible to concentrate with Nick sitting there, sipping his tea—impossible to judge what he was thinking from the cool, yet shuttered expression on his dark face.

He studied her with something approaching amusement as she slammed the flat of her hand down on the kitchen table in a temper as she mis-hit the keyboard yet again.

'Perhaps you'd better stop that for the day?' he suggested. 'You aren't supposed to sit up half the night working, you know.'

She set her lips into a determined line. 'But I'm aiming for a distinction,' she told him.

'And I'm very pleased to hear it. But even chasers of distinctions must eat.' He glanced at his wrist watch. 'And I'm hungry, aren't you?'

She pulled a face. 'I am, but...'

'Mmm?'

She leaned back against the hard kitchen chair. 'I know you said you'd teach me how to cook...'

'And?'

'Well, I'm really keen to learn, Nick...'

'But?'

'After sitting in class all day, I don't know if I can face another lesson right now.'

'That's good,' he responded. 'Because neither can I. I've had—as they say in all the best clichés—a hard day at the office!'

A brief wistfulness stole over her. When he said something like that, he made the two of them sound almost…well, almost… She cleared her throat hastily. 'It looks like sandwiches, then?'

He shuddered. 'You aren't getting out of it that easily.'

'But I can't cook!'

'*Yet!*' he affirmed sternly, and he plucked a fat book from a shelf beside him. 'I know you can't. So you can do what you're good at.' He smiled at her puzzled expression and handed her the telephone directory. 'You can ring out for a take-away!'

For the first time that she could remember, Abigail's life had structure and routine.

Even the boarding-school she had attended had been 'progressive', with pupils encouraged to 'express themselves' in whatever way they chose, which had been the worst possible thing for a girl like Abigail. A fragmented and peculiar childhood had left a teenager who was crying out for some affectionate but firm handling and a little stability.

Well, now she had it.

And she loved it!

She loved catching the bus in the morning, and got up especially early to do so. It was much slower than the tube, because there were always queues of traffic in the clogged city streets, but she enjoyed sitting on the top deck and watching the London morning unfold before her.

She worked harder than anyone else on her course, but then she had more to prove than anyone else.

The evenings had evolved into a gloriously easy and laid-back pattern. They ate take-aways and then they played Scrabble or watched a video.

And if Abigail found herself longing for him to kiss her again, then she knew that a romantic entanglement could ruin things.

Or at least that was what she tried to tell herself.

On Thursday night, towards the end of her first week, Nick arrived home, his black hair spattered with raindrops, and yawned. 'I'm sick of take-aways,' he said as he propped up his umbrella against the wall.

She looked up questioningly from her textbook, glad for the opportunity to take a break from the rather boringly entitled, *English Usage in the Office*. 'And?'

'And I've booked a table for seven-thirty. A little early, I know, but we can't have your work suffering, now, can we? So go and get ready, Abby.'

She stared at him open-mouthed, the reality of having supper with him in a *restaurant* suddenly hitting her, and she felt a huge bubble of excitement well up inside her. But it isn't a date, she told herself fiercely. It's just supper.

'Okay,' she agreed, and sped off to her bedroom to

change, telling herself that she must have sounded like the most pathetic wimp of all time.

Most of the clothes she possessed she rejected immediately as being too over the top. Orlando had liked her to wear dresses which got her noticed, but, now that she had been reminded of Nick's reaction to her skirt all those years ago, she did not imagine that he would take very kindly to one of the extravagant pieces of nothing which dominated her wardrobe.

In the end, her choice was made out of necessity. She came out of the bedroom struggling to do up the zip on a dark blue velvet sheath, which emphasised the pale, creamy skin of her shoulders.

Nick was waiting for her. 'Here, let me,' he said smoothly, and slowly slid the zip into place.

Had he noticed her shiver? she wondered. And, if he had, surely he would put it down to the winter night and not that soft caress as his finger had inadvertently brushed against her bare spine.

'You look wonderful,' he said quietly as she turned round to face him.

'Do I?' She tried to keep the delight from her voice. She had piled her hair up on top of her head, in an unaccustomedly sophisticated style, and secured it with a dark blue pin which matched her dress.

She smoothed the velvet down over her hips, glancing down with a rueful look of horror at the slight swell of her belly. 'Half my clothes don't fit me any more,' she grumbled. 'Since I've been living here, I must have put on at least two kilos!'

'Good,' he said unrepentantly, taking her black velvet swing-coat from her and holding it open. 'You needed to. Now let's go.'

The restaurant he took her to was entirely unexpected, but perhaps she should have been able to predict by now that his choice was likely to be surprising.

It was about as different from the kind of place she had become used to eating out in during her marriage as it was possible to imagine. It was not a place just to see or be seen in.

Relatively small, it was traditionally Italian and packed to bursting. The *maître d'hôtel* guided them through the tables until they were seated in the window, overlooking the night-time Thames as it ran slickly and blackly by.

'People come here to enjoy the food,' Nick told her as she studied the menu greedily.

'And the atmosphere,' she added, glancing around the buzzing room, which included a couple of large family groups.

His mouth softened a fraction as he observed a toddler making messy work of an enormous ice-cream. 'Well, yes!'

He waited until they were settled with a dark, berry-flavoured wine and a dish of olives before he said, 'So tell me what you like best about college.'

She told him about her fellow students, the majority of whom were school-leavers, and mostly female. But there was also a deep-sea diver who had decided to write a book about his experiences, and therefore needed to know how to type.

'Oh, and there's a grandmother of three. She says

she's fed up with sitting around and baking all day and she's aiming to be someone's PA—perhaps she could work for *you*, Nick!' She dimpled. 'She says that age should be no obstacle to whatever you want to do in life!' She stopped suddenly, conscious that she had been monopolising the conversation with her rather dull little anecdotes about what had happened in class that day, when he had probably been dealing with all kinds of bigwigs!

'I'm sorry,' she said awkwardly, 'if I'm boring you.'

'I can assure you that if you had been, then I should not have been such an attentive listener,' he contradicted firmly. He sipped his wine and the glass cast ruby shadows over the sculpted hollows created by his cheekbones. 'Stop apologising, Abby. I'm not Orlando. I *enjoy* your company.'

She went pink. 'Do you?'

'Mmm.' He bit into an olive.

'But you didn't always?'

Their eyes met for a long moment. 'You often used to infuriate me,' he said. 'When you were growing up, I found you headstrong and stubborn—'

'Because I refused to bend to your will?'

'Perhaps there was an element of that in it,' he admitted. 'Although I like to think that I was motivated by concern for your welfare. I couldn't understand why your mother and Philip just seemed to let you run wild.'

Abigail shrugged. 'It seemed like freedom at the time; it's only with hindsight that you realise it wasn't the *right* kind of freedom.' She twirled the stem of her wineglass between her fingers, watching the pink-dappled shadows move on the tablecloth. 'I think they did their best, but quite frankly my mother wasn't really interested in children, and Philip was far too old and unconnected to know what I really needed.'

'That's all in the past now.' His green gaze was steady. 'And you sound as though you're enjoying yourself at the moment?'

'Oh, I am,' Abigail agreed. At this precise moment she couldn't ever remember feeling so happy, but Nick was talking about her college course, not the fact that he was her partner for the evening!

She watched two plates of melon and parma ham being balanced precariously *en route* to their table. She looked at Nick seriously as the waiter put the dishes down before them. 'It's difficult to explain what college is like.' She speared a succulent wedge of fruit. 'I feel…well, *ordinary* for once in my life. And you can't imagine how good that is.'

'Oh, I think that I probably can,' he demurred drily. 'I imagine that it must be a little like leaving behind a burden which had become intolerable over the years.'

Her eyes met his over the top of her glass and she swallowed a lump of longing. Was he always like this? This understanding? And why had she been so blind to it before?

Of course she ate far more than she had intended, and ordered a pudding—even though she had vowed not to at the beginning of the meal.

Nick laughed as he watched her ruefully gazing at the portion of chocolate trifle which had been placed before her. 'I think perhaps I should save you from your sins,' he murmured, and leant forward. 'Don't you?'

Abigail held her breath while she fed him a spoonful of trifle, her heart thudding dangerously as he let his tongue slide along his lips to lick off an errant trace of cream. Was that a deliberately provocative movement? she wondered briefly. And then decided that it probably wasn't. She thought that quite seriously Nick could even make blowing his nose look sexy!

Beneath the thankfully heavy material of her velvet dress, she could feel her nipples prickle into alarmingly sensitive life and a kind of pleasurable ache start deep within her. 'More?' she queried breathlessly.

'Mmm. Please.'

Abigail fed him the rest of her chocolate pudding in what, for her, was the single most erotic act in her life to date. Her hands were damp with excitement, her pulse still racing as the spoon clattered into the empty dish because her hand was shaking so much.

When the waiter finally took the plate away she did not know whether to weep with gratitude or frustration. She could scarcely bear to look Nick in the eyes. Had he guessed, she wondered, just what effect he was having on her?

She escaped to the powder-room and yanked all her hair from out of its top-knot, brushing it energetically until it fell in a gleaming, honey-coloured curtain all the way down her back.

She could see that there was coffee on the table, and as she threaded her way through the tables she was aware of Nick's eyes fixed on her; there was an odd sort of silence when she sat down.

'You've let your hair down,' he said eventually.

'Yes.'

'Why?'

She could hardly tell him that it was because she was flushed with what even *she* knew was sexual excitement. That, as well as the red blotches all over her neck being unbecoming, they were also a dead giveaway of the effect he had been having on her all evening!

'It felt constricting,' she lied, and then, because she didn't know how much longer she could carry on sitting opposite him without doing something stupid, like leaning across the table to kiss him, she pretended to yawn. 'Can we go home soon?' she asked him. 'I have an early start in the morning.'

If he knew that her tiredness was manufactured, then his face gave no hint of it. 'Of course,' he replied blandly, and indicated for the bill.

Abigail was glad to get outside in the fresh air. The earlier rain had blown away all the clouds, which had given way to a bright, clear night with a star-studded sky.

They drove home in silence, and it wasn't until they were standing in the entrance hall, and Nick had closed the front door behind them, that Abigail turned to him with the question which had been nagging uncomfortably at the back of her mind all evening.

'Nick?'

He turned to look down at her. 'Abby?'

'Can I ask you something?'

He studied her face for a long moment. 'Ask away,' he said. 'Though if it's a question which requires a protracted answer then we might be better going upstairs to the sitting-room, mightn't we?'

'I guess so.'

But by the time she had settled herself on one of the long sofas and was facing him, her nerve had almost failed her. Almost. But not quite.

He had taken off his jacket and his tie, and undone the top two buttons of his shirt. As he leaned back against the soft cushions he looked the picture of elegant relaxation.

It really wasn't fair, thought Abigail a touch despairingly, as she tried very hard not to let her gaze rove over his lean, rangy body.

Did he *have* to wear a silk shirt so fine, she wondered, that it gave intoxicating glimpses of that magnificent torso? Was he aware that she could quite clearly make out that flat, hard abdomen? Did he not realise that she was yearning to be in his arms again?

She gave her head an impatient little shake of denial—totally unprepared for the way she was feeling.

She had really thought that Orlando had turned her off men for good, and yet Nick had awakened all the responses she had thought killed for ever—the lack of which had made her feel only half a woman.

Yet the desire she felt for Nick was not quite the liberation she might have imagined it to be. Because lurking at the back of her mind was the awful fear that it might never be consummated, and that she might once more slip back into that stultifying state of feeling only half alive...

He had not touched her since that shattering kiss on her bed, when he had railed against her and accused her of being like her mother. Did he still think that? Or had they been empty, angry words, fuelled by her freezing up at precisely the wrong time?

Had her momentary mental and physical withdrawal offended his prowess as a lover? Or was that how a man like Nick Harrington usually operated? she wondered. Tantalising and then retreating? Was withholding pleasure the ultimate enticement? So that a woman would dwell on the sheer potency of his kiss over and over again, until she was left too weak with longing to resist him?

She might never know the answer to *that*, but there was a question she was perfectly justified in asking him. She looked at him across the stylish sitting-room.

'When we were at the house and you suggested I was as promiscuous as my mother had been...' She noticed him flinch very slightly, but, quite honestly, she felt that he deserved to feel bad about what he had said to her. 'Did you mean that, Nick?'

He was silent for a moment, and then, to her astonishment, he got up and came to sit beside her on the sofa, taking her hand between his in a curiously impartial gesture. 'No, of course, I didn't mean it,' he said in a low voice. 'And I've already apologised to you, Abby.'

'Then why *say* it, if you didn't mean it?'

He sighed. 'I said it because I was angry, and...'

She looked into his eyes, so exotically green tonight. 'And what?'

'Frustrated,' he admitted reluctantly. 'Because I badly wanted to make love to you—'

'D-Did you?' she whispered.

His mouth tightened. 'You know damned well I did! Don't be naive with me, Abby, you were a married woman, after all!'

Fear gripped her, but Abigail deliberately chose to ignore it. Because if she gave in to it then that would be Orlando's bitter legacy to her—that she would never be able to respond to another man.

She stared down at her hand, which lay so acquiescent and pale in Nick's, and forced herself to challenge him. 'And is that how you always respond to women you want to make love to? By casting them aside and then insulting them?'

'It was the verbal equivalent of a cold shower,' he said. 'And unforgivable. I'm sorry.'

She slowly nodded her head. 'But you still haven't answered my question.'

'I didn't think I needed to,' he said softly. 'But, no, Abby. I don't usually cast them aside and then insult them, as you so sweetly put it.'

This hurt. Badly. 'Then why?' she demanded. 'Why me?'

'Because I hadn't intended to make love to you in

the first place. I came to bring you tea, but you were asleep, and you looked very beautiful and very alluring. You looked peaceful, too, and I felt that you needed peace more than anything else at that moment. So I didn't even try to wake you, just sat watching you sleep, and then, when you stirred...' his voice deepened into an unwilling whisper which was harshened by desire '...I came to you in spite of myself.'

She wondered if he had intended this admission to sound quite so insulting. Because it did. Terribly. 'And?'

'And it was something of a relief when you seemed to have second thoughts and tensed up on me. It forced me to take stock of what I was doing. And stop.'

She forced herself to ask another question. 'And if it had been anyone else, then would you have stopped?'

He hesitated, as if reluctant to answer her. Did he sense that his reply might hurt her? 'No.'

Abigail's skin iced up. 'Even if they had—had tensed up, too?'

He regarded her thoughtfully. 'That hasn't happened to me before, but there are ways of getting over tension, you know, Abby.'

'You mean...seduction?'

'I mean that an experienced man should be able to make the woman relax, so that any tension she feels will melt away.'

'But you didn't feel the urge to make me relax?'

He smiled. 'I felt the urge very strongly, but I also

felt it very important that I should resist giving in to it.'

'You have a great deal of self-control,' said Abigail, trying to keep the disappointment out of her voice.

He shook his head, a wry expression on his face. 'I didn't particularly enjoy exercising it—not on that occasion, certainly.'

If living with Orlando had taught her only one thing, it was that the only healthy way in which to live your life was honestly. 'So why did you?' she asked.

He raised his black brows into two arrogant arches. 'You're very persistent,' he murmured, and let go of her hand quite suddenly. Abigail was alarmed by how much she missed that warm contact of skin against skin. His skin. 'Because it was the wrong time. And the wrong place.'

She digested this in silence, aware that her questions might be classified as intrusive but spurred on by a powerful need to know. 'And now?' she asked.

He smiled, but she could sense the sudden tension in him. 'That is what is known as throwing down the gauntlet,' he told her softly. 'You mean, do I still want to make love to you?'

She blushed at something she read in his eyes, at the knowledge of how frankly they were talking. At how he had managed to turn the conversation around to make it sound as though she was propositioning him! 'I didn't mean that at all!' she exclaimed, backtracking like mad.

'Oh, come on, Abby,' he remonstrated softly. 'I found your honesty quite refreshing—don't go all coy on me now. And, yes, of course I want to make love to you. You are a very beautiful young woman, and you have a way of looking at me sometimes which makes me feel positively...' But he checked himself with a shake of his dark head.

'Positively what?' she ventured.

'Making love to you would be fraught with emotional difficulties,' he said at last. 'And they are the last things you need right now...'

But his words tailed off as he took in her pale, strained face and the glittering darkness of her eyes. He hesitated for just a fraction, and then, with an almost angry little moan of capitulation, he bent his head and captured her parted mouth by storm. Soundlessly her arms went around him, as if she had finally come home.

She clung to him as if for life itself, while he proceeded to kiss her as if it were the first time he had ever kissed a woman.

Or maybe the last.

Exhilaration and relief flooded her veins as her body instantly responded to him in an explosion of excitement, because part of her had been afraid that the other day had been nothing more than wishful thinking. But it was true! He *could* make her feel this good. And oh, *oh*, it was good!

She let her tongue make snaking little movements against his, and the shudder that this provoked in him made her melt. She felt a heavy, sweet stirring tugging deep at the heart of her, but, just when her breasts had begun to clamour to be allowed some of the attention that he was giving to her lips, he wrenched his mouth away from hers.

Her hands continued to clasp at the broad bank of his shoulders, as though he were the rock on which she depended, and he gently removed them, as if he were extricating limpets from a rock. Then he stood up and moved away from the sofa, not speaking until he had control of his breath once more.

Abigail stared up at him, feeling a mixture of dismay and regret. She couldn't believe that she had been so pushy! And with *Nick* of all people!

Yet the dismay at his *stopping* making love to her was far greater than any regret she might have felt about bringing the subject up in the first place.

She observed the pulse that beat so frantically at the base of his temple, and his eyes which did not look green at all just now, but black as jet. And as night. At that moment they conjured up all things which were dark and mysterious and powerful. She shivered with longing.

He lifted his arm to glance rather pointedly down at his wrist watch, but Abigail could sense that he was holding onto his composure with an effort.

'I'm going to shower,' he told her. 'And you'd better go to bed.' His eyes glittered with warning. 'We wouldn't want you to be late for college in the morning, now, would we, Abby?'

CHAPTER EIGHT

THE following morning Abigail awoke early to an empty house. Nick had left a rather terse note perched against the teapot saying that he had gone to Cambridge for the day and that he couldn't say for certain what time he would be home. It was abrupt and to the point, and it told her quite clearly that last night was not intended to be repeated.

And although Abigail was disappointed—of course she was—in a way it came as something of a relief to know that at least now she knew exactly where she stood. He had made it patently clear last night that, although he was still attracted to her, he had no intention of giving in to that desire.

Whatever his reasons for that—and part of Abigail recognised that he would probably find it unpalatable to become the lover of someone he had always considered spoilt and privileged—then those reasons must be respected. For her own pride as much as anything else.

Because she certainly wasn't going to throw herself at him *again*, she thought haughtily as she defiantly covered the dark shadows beneath her eyes with an extra splodge of foundation. And she wasn't going to sit around at home and mope either!

So she started staying later at college in the evenings, and quickly made friends with another girl on her course named Hannah, who lived in a tiny flat close to Shepherd's Bush tube station.

It was Hannah's first time in London—she'd been born in Wales—and in a way it was Abigail's, too. Because the London life she had known with Orlando had been the type which relied on limitless funds, and now, like Hannah, she had the bare minimum. There wasn't a single person from Abigail's former life whom she wished to see; she realised that all their 'friends' had been Orlando's friends, and she vowed never to let a man run her life quite so ruthlessly again.

She and Hannah spent every lunchtime exploring the city on a shoestring budget, and it surprised Abigail just how much fun it could be. They went to nothing that wasn't free, and sometimes just took a ride on the tube for the hell of it—buying a ticket to a place that neither had been to before and exploring. Soon they began to move around the city like true natives.

One evening, Abigail was lying on the floor of the sitting-room, poring over a brochure, when she heard Nick arrive home, and she felt her shoulders automatically stiffen up with tension. After their restaurant meal and the subsequent talk, which had ended with Nick pushing her away so abruptly, their evenings were now largely spent apart.

He had taken to working late, too, and when they *did* meet—for meals, which he now seemed disinclined to teach her how to cook—he always accorded her the kind of cool politeness he might to a maiden aunt. And how she hated it!

Hearing the front door being slammed shut loudly, Abigail pretended to read her brochure, when in reality she was listening to him clattering around downstairs while her heart beat out a wild tattoo in her ears.

Nick appeared at the door of the sitting-room carrying two glasses of wine and raised one dark, elegant eyebrow at her. 'Like one?'

Relations had been so strained recently that she was tempted to say no thank you, as a means of carrying on the war which had been raging between them rather than refusing because she didn't want a drink. But then she saw the dark shadows under his eyes, the lines of strain etched on his gorgeous face, and her heart turned over.

'Thanks.' She took the glass from him and sipped the wine. 'You look absolutely awful,' she said, as she watched him sink gratefully onto one of the roomy sofas and kick his shoes off.

'Thanks,' he said drily, giving her a glimmer of a smile before taking a deep swallow of his wine and resting his head on the back of the sofa.

'Bad day?'

'Oh, wonderful. The financial director of the company I'm investigating hasn't exactly been falling over himself to be interviewed. Now I discover why. He's been creaming off the profits for the past two years. Mind you, he's covered his tracks very well,' he added, in a voice of reluctant admiration.

Abigail sat up. 'Will he go to prison?'

He smiled. 'He may. If they ever catch him. Which I doubt. He flew out of Heathrow early this morning on a false passport, taking one of his mistresses with him. But crime is so boring, Abby—let's talk about something else.' He glanced down at the slim catalogue she was reading. 'What's that?'

'Oh, it's from the Tate. I went there at lunchtime. With Hannah.'

Nick nodded. He had met a wide-eyed Hannah once, when Abigail had invited her back for supper, and had liked her. 'To the new exhibition?'

She looked shocked. 'Good heavens, no! We only go to the bit that's free. The exhibition you pay for.'

He looked momentarily exasperated. 'Abby, aren't you taking your fierce new independence a tad too far? I told you, I'm perfectly prepared to give you an allowance which would easily cover going to exhibitions. The theatre, too,' he added.

'And I've thanked you, but no, thanks!' Abigail declared. 'Hannah couldn't afford to do those things on her budget, and she certainly wouldn't let me treat her.'

There was silence while he considered this. 'Might she let *me* treat her?'

A bolt of pure jealousy shot through Abigail. 'You mean you want to take her out?'

He gave a slow smile. 'And you, you idiot. Ask her.'

So the following weekend he spoilt them rotten.

They visited the Tower of London and Hampton Court Palace, took a breathtaking river cruise and spent an afternoon at Madame Tussaud's and the Planetarium.

Afterwards they were thoroughly exhausted, though not *too* exhausted to sit through a spellbinding performance of Les Misérables, where Nick had miraculously managed to obtain the best seats in the house at short notice.

Hannah was impressed. She had just finished putting on a slick of lipstick in the theatre cloakroom during the interval, and met Abigail's eyes in the mirror. 'He's wonderful,' she said fervently.

'Who?'

'Nick, of course.'

Abigail had opened her mouth to deny it when the prospect of lying about her feelings yet again became too much, and her face crumpled. 'I know he is,' she admitted miserably.

Hannah looked at her sternly. 'Are you in love with him?'

'I don't know.' Abigail shook her head distractedly. 'Yes, I do! Of course I love him! I think I've always loved him. Loving him isn't the problem, Hannah; most people would love him if they knew him. He's an easy man to love.'

'I can imagine,' said Hannah, trying to keep the twinge of envy out of her voice. 'So what are you doing about it?'

'About what?'

'About snaring him, of course!'

'He isn't the kind of man who would approve of being ensnared,' said Abigail primly.

'Few men do,' commented Hannah, with a sagacity beyond her years. 'But it's been going on since time began.'

Abigail shook her head. 'I don't want him unless he wants me—without any game-playing or arm-twisting. I had enough of that during my marriage,' she said bitterly.

'And *does* he want you?'

'He...' She blushed.

'Obviously, yes,' observed Hannah drily.

'He says he does.' Abigail hesitated. 'But I think he only means in a physical sense.'

Hannah almost dropped her handbag. 'And you're objecting to a man like that wanting you in a physical sense?' she queried incredulously. 'You must be *mad*!'

But Abigail wanted so much more than that. She wanted the whole works. She wanted Nick for a lifetime. 'Anyway...' She sniffed. 'He won't make love to me because he says it would be fraught with emotional difficulties.'

Hannah burst out laughing. 'He *must* be in love if he can come out with rubbish like that!' But she sobered at the sight of Abigail's stricken face. 'Let me get this straight. *He* doesn't want you, or says he doesn't. Right?'

'Right,' agreed Abigail wretchedly.

'But I'll bet my last dollar that he doesn't want anyone else to have you, either! Typical dog-in-a-manger attitude of the male sex in general,' she added disparagingly.

'So what do I do?'

'Easy! You make him jealous. See how he reacts if he sees you with another man. Ask one of the lads from college to go along with it. Jason would do it—he's game for anything.' Hannah's eyes darkened lustfully at the prospect of Jason taking part in 'anything'.

'I don't know if I could be that cold-blooded about it,' said Abigail uncertainly.

'Rubbish!' said Hannah. 'Of course you can!'

In the end, Abigail didn't have to; fate played right into her hands on the very last day of the course.

The whole class had come out of the building at five o'clock, all clutching their diplomas—though Abigail had been the only one to gain a distinction. It was already dark, and some early Christmas decorations could be seen glittering in the windows of a nearby pub.

'Let's go for a drink to celebrate,' said Jason, with a sideways smile at Hannah.

'I'm game!' she said, in her lovely, lilting Welsh accent. 'So's Abby, aren't you?' She bent her mouth to whisper in Abigail's ear. 'You leave a message at the house, asking Nick to collect you from the pub. He's kind of old-fashioned, isn't he?'

'Old-fashioned?' asked Abigail indignantly.

'I just mean he's the type of man who wouldn't want a woman travelling on her own in a city at night,' said Hannah, rather wistfully. 'He's bound to want to collect you!'

In the end, about twelve of them convened at the

pub, including the grandmother and the deep-sea diver, who had the younger ones in fits of laughter.

Abigail was enjoying herself so much that she completely forgot about the time, and, when she looked at her watch, she saw that it was almost eight o'clock.

'Help!' she said. 'I'd better ring Nick.'

She dialled the number a little unsteadily. She had only had two glasses of wine, but they had been drunk on an empty stomach.

The phone was snatched up on the second ring.

'Nick?'

'Abby?'

She giggled.

'Where the hell *are* you?'

'In a pub—'

'You surprise me,' he offered sarcastically. 'Who with?'

'Just Hannah,' she replied innocently. 'And...' she let her voice dip seductively '...a friend.'

'Which pub?' he demanded.

'The Black Dog. It's next to the college—'

'Wait there,' he ordered.

'Nick?' But Abigail could hear nothing but the infuriating whine of a disconnected line. She walked back to the table to find Hannah watching her face eagerly.

'Well?'

'He's on his way.'

'Great! Jason will sit next to you and look as though he's hanging onto your every word with ardent fascination!'

'There's no need to make it sound as if he'll have trouble managing it!' returned Abigail, uneasy about the wisdom of playing games with Nick.

Actually, Jason turned out to be very interesting, and, because Abigail was not in the slightest bit interested in him from a romantic point of view, she was uninhibited enough to ask him all kinds of questions about his upbringing, the answers to which, she noticed wryly, Hannah was soaking up like a sponge beside her.

Consequently, Abigail failed to notice the door swing open noisily, but she felt the bitter winter wind which blew in behind it, and looked up to see Nick Harrington striding into the saloon bar.

In fact, Nick's entry into the pub was exactly like a scene from a Western, particularly as he was wearing a pair of faded jeans which looked as though they had been lovingly sprayed on to cover his impressively muscular legs. On top of the jeans he wore a big, cream Aran sweater, and his dark hair was delectably ruffled.

Every pore of his body announced that here was a big, strong, virile male, and every woman in the pub unconsciously sat up a little straighter and sucked in their stomachs.

You could have heard a pin drop, thought Abigail as she watched those mesmeric eyes which burned with emerald fire. Would he storm over and demand that she leave immediately? she wondered dreamily. And then an awful thought occurred to her. What if he was so angry that he punched Jason on the jaw?

With a grimace she pictured the ensuing scene. The police... The ambulance...

'Abigail?'

She looked up to find that he was standing there, an amused smile playing around the corners of his mouth.

'Hi,' he said softly.

'H-hi.'

'Ready to go?' he queried.

Abigail swallowed. This wasn't how it was supposed to happen at all. By now he should be glowering at Jason. 'This is Jason,' she blurted out. 'Jason, this is Nick Harrington.'

To her surprise and annoyance, the two men shook hands.

'Pleased to meet you, Jason,' said Nick. 'How are you, Hannah?'

'Fine,' dimpled Hannah.

'I'd offer you a lift somewhere—'

'No, thanks,' said Hannah hastily. 'We're staying here, aren't we, Jason?'

'We are?' queried Jason, with the rather confused look of a man who was only just realising he had met his match.

It was just very unfortunate that Abigail developed hiccups in the car.

'If you hadn't drunk quite so much...' Nick accused witheringly.

'I haven't!' *Hic!* 'Two glasses of wine, that's all. But no supper,' she added plaintively.

'Try holding your breath,' he advised unsympathetically, as he roared around Hyde Park Corner.

'For how long?'

'Don't tempt me, Abby.'

'But I don't. Do I? That's the trouble.'

'Just shut up,' he told her, not unkindly.

'Are you angry with me?'

'For succeeding in making me dash across London like a madman, convinced that you were about to be sold into slavery?' In the darkness he smiled. 'No, Abby, I'm not angry—perhaps just a little startled by my own reaction.'

And probably regretting it like mad, she thought gloomily.

When they arrived home, Abigail drank endless cups of black coffee and then went upstairs to shower. She felt a million times better when she emerged, with her hair all washed.

She put on a short flounced navy blue skirt, white slouch-socks and a white silk overshirt and then padded downstairs to the sitting-room, where a fire Nick had obviously lit while she was in the shower was beginning to blaze. He was crouched beside it, coaxing the coals into life.

'Are you hungry?' he asked.

She shook her head, and the damp tendrils swung around her neck like snakes, but she didn't know whether it was *that* making her shiver, or the dark, intent look, quite unlike any other she had ever seen, to which Nick was now subjecting her.

'Come and sit over here by the fire,' he instructed.

'And I'll brush your hair for you.' He held out his hand for the brush she was holding.

'But—'

'Just do it, Abby. Would you?'

She handed it over and he sat down on the floor behind her. Lifting the heavy strands into his hand, he began to brush. 'Don't you know that masterful men have gone out of fashion?' she grumbled.

She could hear the amusement in his voice as he said, 'I don't think so.'

It was heaven. The warmth of the burgeoning fire was as hypnotic as the rhythmic strokes that he swept through her hair. She wanted to lean back against him, but resisted. After all, she had expressly told herself she was *not* going to fling herself at him again.

'Relax,' he urged. 'For God's sake, Abby, just relax.'

And the moment she eased herself back against the powerful strength of his thighs, she felt all the tension ebb away.

When he'd finished, he moved to kneel down in front of her, laying the hairbrush down on the carpet between them and capturing her with that hypnotic gaze of his.

'That's how I like you best,' he said suddenly. 'Without a scrap of make-up on your face and your hair all loose and free.'

'Without artifice, you mean?' she asked him in surprise.

'As nature intended,' he affirmed softly.

It had not been like that with Orlando, Abigail

thought suddenly, her face crumpling with the memory.

Orlando had wanted her gilded and painted—wearing the kind of dress which you needed to be poured into, with the make-up thick on her face. Like a doll, as Nick had said. A pretty accessory. And she had allowed him to dictate those likes and dislikes to her—that was the thing which most appalled her. Her total willingness to be moulded.

'Did you love him?' Nick asked suddenly, and Abigail's head jerked up as she stared back at him with a bewildered question in her eyes.

'Orlando,' he elaborated. 'I mean, in the beginning? You must have felt something when you married him. Did you love him then?'

Had he read her thoughts? Or did her face give her away? She stared down, almost dispassionately, and realised that her hands were shaking.

'I thought I did,' she answered slowly. 'But I think I was dazzled by him more than anything else. He was the first person who I thought loved me unconditionally...' Her fixed smile wavered and she forced herself to look up and meet that quizzical green gaze. 'But of course he was a very good actor.'

'Want to tell me about it?' he asked softly.

She sensed Nick's need to know what lay behind her marriage without really understanding what motivated it. But she also recognised that talking about it was a way of letting the memories go for good.

'I wasn't working hard enough at school,' she admitted. 'And I got in with a bad crowd. I was just drifting along. And then Orlando exploded into my life.' Abigail sighed. 'Philip and my mother were travelling, as usual, and had sent me on a school skiing trip. The future seemed very uncertain and frightening. It was an easy way out—to believe myself in love with Orlando. To allow him to take care of me so that I wouldn't have to do it myself. I accept that now.

'After my mother and Philip were killed—' her eyes closed briefly as she remembered '—Orlando just kind of took over, really. You were working in the Far East, and Orlando gave me a shoulder to cry on. He was immensely kind to me—motivated by an eye for the main chance, I guess. But when you're young and alone and think you're in love...well...' She grimaced. 'That proposal of marriage seemed like the answer to all my dreams.'

Nick's face had darkened with anger and a kind of self-recrimination. 'I was held up for days. If only I had got back sooner. If only I had stopped you,' he breathed fiercely.

'You can't ever say "if only", —that's one thing I *have* learnt. And you *tried*,' pointed out Abigail. 'Remember? You tried and you failed.'

He shook his dark head. 'No, Abby. If I *had* tried, I mean *really* tried, then I would not have failed.'

Her heart was in her mouth as she slowly raised her face to his. 'And how would you have done that?'

'Like this,' he murmured, and leaned forward to kiss her.

It was a slow kiss. A deliberate kiss. A territorial

kiss—and it was what Abigail had secretly craved from him for longer than she could remember. She realised that now.

She felt her heart lurch painfully in her chest as he drew her into the circle of his arms, smoothing her newly brushed hair down with his hands as his mouth continued its sweet foray. Her body melted towards him, her nipples hardening against his chest, her hands instinctively moving to lock themselves around his neck as he deepened the kiss.

'Oh, Nick,' she breathed.

That kiss made her dizzy, and it made her weak, and yet when he stopped kissing her she felt just as debilitated. But he had only stopped so that he could sink down onto the carpet, pulling her down so that they were lying side by side, their faces close. His green eyes were as enigmatic as Abigail had ever seen them, and she was absolutely terrified that he was going to change his mind again. She couldn't bear that, not this time.

Boldly, she captured his face between the palms of her hands and kissed him back.

She heard him sigh, an odd, desperate, almost resigned kind of sigh, as though she had just given him an answer to something he had not needed to put into words. And perhaps she had, for her action had subtly altered things. His kisses became more demanding, tinged with a stark hunger that was new to Abigail. Suddenly the kiss was not enough, although it was as intimate a kiss as she had ever experienced.

He seemed to sense it, too, because he began to

unbutton her shirt, a soft smile playing at the corners of his mouth as he did so. His eyes asked her a question as his fingers deftly began to slip the buttons free, and she knew that if she gave the slightest indication he would stop.

But she didn't want him to stop. She wanted this feeling to go on and on. She wanted the honeyed ache she felt at the fork of her thighs to intensify, and then...

Every button of her shirt was now undone, and he pushed each half of the fabric aside, gazing down at her breasts with a curiously intent expression, at the delicate white lace which did little to conceal them from him.

'Now,' he said lazily, and lowered his head to suckle one nipple through the silk and lace.

It was so unexpected. She nearly cried aloud as she felt the tip peak violently against the wetness of his tongue, and as the aching within her became almost too much to bear her body began to arch helplessly towards him.

Weakly, her hand fluttered up with the intention of unbuttoning *his* shirt, but he halted her tremulous fingers with a warm, caressing clasp, lifting his head from her breast.

'Easy, sweetheart,' he soothed softly.

Dazed, she let her hand fall, too intent on the sensations he was provoking to do anything other than lie back and enjoy them.

Desire washed slowly over her, deep and heady as

any drug. She felt it flooding through her veins, rich and sweet and irresistible.

'I thought…'

'Mmm,' he said, between kisses. 'What did you think, Abby?'

She wasn't sure she could remember. 'You making love to me…'

'Mmm?'

'Would be…' She fought for breath, for sanity, but when he was voluptuously licking her nipple like that, it wasn't just difficult, it was almost impossible. 'Would be fraught with emotional difficulties,' she managed.

'Did I say that?' he murmured. 'Did I really?'

She gave a little moan as he slipped his hand beneath the silken shirt to unclip her bra with a sureness of touch she didn't find in the least bit intimidating. And she made a tiny moue of relief as her aching, swollen breasts were released from their confinement.

He slid the shirt from around her shoulders so that it slithered unnoticed to the floor. The bra joined it and she was naked to the waist, wearing nothing but the little flounced skirt and the slouch socks, and she felt a primitive sense of triumph as a small shudder racked through his giant frame.

'Oh, sweetheart,' he murmured. 'Sweetheart. Don't you know that I've barely slept since you arrived, imagining you in my arms like this? So near…and yet…'

He started kissing her all over again, gradually driving her into such a state of expectancy that she really thought that she might die from pleasure. She clung even more tightly to him—particularly when his fingers began to slowly trickle their way up the inside of her leg, seeming to take for ever before they reached the top of her thigh.

'Nick,' she moaned, aware that he was leading her down an uncharted path—and she found she was suddenly desperate to reach the end of it.

'What?' he whispered. 'What is it?'

'Please…' she begged him, without knowing what she was pleading for.

'No,' he whispered provocatively. 'Not yet.'

She was utterly breathless, and her heart was pounding as one finger flicked lightly back and forth to graze teasingly over the moist silk of her panties. And when he moved the fabric aside to touch her swollen, sensitive flesh she *did* gasp, moving her body restlessly, seeking something so beautifully elusive that part of her felt scared, in case these sensations were simply the product of her fevered imagination. And it would all come to nothing.

He felt her shifting, seeking movements as he continued to caress and stroke her, and drew his lips away from her mouth for a moment, his gaze raking over her, taking in her closed eyes, her flushed cheeks and the tiny beads of moisture which studded her forehead.

'I think, my darling, that I'd better take you to bed, don't you?' His hand stilled and she could have wept.

She shook her head distractedly, not wanting to lose this feeling, terrified that in the short trip from the sitting-room to the bedroom it would elude her for ever...

'No,' she whispered. 'Don't stop. Please don't stop.'

His eyes narrowed. 'Don't stop what, Abby? This?'

'Yes.'

'Or this?'

'*Yes!*'

'Or this?'

'Oh, God, yes!' She tensed for a moment, poised on a knife-edge, and then a deliciously wicked feeling of inevitability began to wash over her. 'Oh, Nick... Nick...*Nick!*' His name was torn from her lips one last time in a broken sob as the sweet waves of abandonment obliterated everything. And the reality, she thought in dazed disbelief, eclipsed even her own most far-fetched flights of fantasy.

In a stunned haze, she listened to the slowing of her heart, too lethargic to raise a murmur when he scooped her up and carried her upstairs to her bedroom.

When reason returned she was lying on the bed, cradled against his chest. Her cheeks were wet and he was stroking her hair very, very gently.

'Nick—'

'Shh,' he soothed. 'It's all right.'

'It's never—'

He held her a little bit away from him, so that she could see the tenderness which softened his hard features. 'You don't have to explain, Abby. It's okay, I know.'

'No, you don't,' she said miserably.

He pushed a strand of hair out of her eyes. 'That you just had your first orgasm?'

She closed her eyes in despair.

'Don't you know how much pleasure it gave *me*, too, sweetheart?'

If she kept her eyes closed she could pretend that everything was all right. That she was warm and protected and nothing could ever hurt her again.

'It's okay, Abby,' he murmured. 'Everything's going to be okay.'

She was so drowsy with the aftermath of pleasure that for a moment she could almost believe him.

And, to her astonishment, she found herself drifting off to sleep.

CHAPTER NINE

WHEN Abby awoke it was morning. She was naked beneath the covers, and... She stiffened...

So was Nick!

Her heart racing, she listened to the regular sound of his breathing, and was sliding towards the edge of the bed to make her escape when a deep, silky voice challenged, 'Going somewhere, sweetheart?'

She blanched. 'To the b-bathroom,' she stuttered, giving him an embarrassed half-glance over her shoulder.

He propped himself up on the batch of pillows, looking disgustingly healthy, the duvet dramatically white against his gloriously tanned chest. 'Hurry up, then,' he murmured.

He looked so gorgeous and so relaxed and so—so *easy* with the whole situation that the part of her that wasn't longing for him absolutely quailed.

Just the sight of him could start that aching again, and yet she was petrified. She wasn't stupid. Last night he had pleasured her most conclusively and had then displayed a remarkable degree of self-control and understanding by letting her fall asleep.

This morning, though, there would be no excuse...

He leaned over and planted a kiss on her shoulder. 'Abby,' he grumbled against her bare skin, 'will you stop dithering and just *go*? Because I want to kiss you, and once I start kissing you I don't intend to stop for a very long time.'

Like a scalded cat, she leapt up off the bed and hurried into the bathroom where she spent ages— brushing her teeth so hard that she was certain she must have scraped half the enamel off them, and then stroking the brush through her hair until it gleamed.

Her dark blue silk kimono was hanging on the back of the door and she put it on gratefully. She didn't know what he would think of that, but right now she didn't care. Because there was no way that she could face prancing back out there completely naked.

When she really could not put it off any longer, she pushed open the door into the bedroom to find Nick leaning against the pillows, his hands cradling his dark head, a watchful expression stealing over his face as unflickering green eyes took in the tightly knotted kimono.

'Come here,' he said softly.

She felt torn between wanting to run into his arms and wanting to turn tail and flee from the bedroom. She walked slowly towards him, then sat down awkwardly and met his assessing gaze.

He didn't touch her. Did he sense her terror and confusion? Instead, he said the last thing in the world she would have expected.

'I want to marry you, Abby.'

She froze as she stared at him in horror, all the blood draining from her face.

He frowned. 'Not quite the reaction I was hoping for,' he said drily.

Fear made her attack him, like a trapped animal lashing out at its rescuer. 'And what reaction was that, Nick? That I would fall down on my knees in gratitude?'

His eyes narrowed. 'Gratitude? That would imply that I was doing you a favour,' he said, a cool note stealing into his voice.

'When in reality I'm doing *you* a favour?' she shot back.

'And just what is that supposed to mean?' he asked in a dangerously quiet voice.

'It means that you're the ultimate control freak!' she yelled at him.

'What?'

'Yes! Just that! I've worked it all out!'

'Have you?' he enunciated carefully. 'Perhaps you'd care to share it with me?'

'Right!' She took a deep breath. 'You're thirty and you've reached a stage in your life when you've decided that you really ought to get married and settle down.'

The look of curiosity in his eyes had given way to one of marked irritation. 'Do carry on,' he drawled. 'This makes *fascinating* listening.'

'Women love you because you're rich and successful and gorgeous—but that's not quite enough, is it, Nick? Because in the back of your mind you always wonder whether they would love you without the trappings.' She drew a deep breath. 'And you trust *me* because I've known you a long time and because there has always been some kind of sexual chemistry between us. Am I right?'

'Go on,' he said.

'So, perhaps I made good raw material for a wife— except, of course, for the troublesome elements of my character that the high-and-mighty Nick Harrington didn't approve of. You thought me rich and spoiled, didn't you, Nick?'

'And weren't you?' he queried coolly.

That did it! His calmly critical query convinced her that she was justified in her accusations. 'Maybe I was!' Her eyes spat midnight fire at him. 'So you set about improving me, didn't you? As if I were a bloody car you were doing up to sell! Abby can't earn a living—well, then, we'll teach her how to! Abby can't survive without a massive expense account— then let's make her! Abby's never had an orgasm—'

'That's *enough*!' he yelled.

'You think you can just play bloody Pygmalion!' she sobbed. 'Well, you can't! If I marry again it will be for all the right reasons this time. For love—'

'Abby—'

'No!' she sobbed. 'Don't tell me you love me, Nick, not now—not just so that you can get what you want! If I married you now, then wouldn't I be just a pretty accessory again—the way I was with Orlando? Wouldn't I be staying with you for security as much as anything else? How can you love someone who has never had to stand on her own two feet? How can I ever learn to love myself when I've always depended on somebody else to support me?' she finished brokenly.

Without a word he got out of bed, and Abby averted her eyes from the magnificence of his naked body—but not before she had seen that he was aroused. Very aroused. With his back to her, he seemed to spend a hell of a long time zipping up his jeans, but when he turned back to her, his face was quite calm.

'You're absolutely right, of course.'

Her heart sank. Had she secretly been hoping that he would play masterful again? Haul her into his arms and kiss every last doubt from her mind?

'The question is where do we go from here?' he mused, seeming lost in thought, moving to look out of the window at the complicated fretwork the overlapping branches of the trees made. After a couple of moments he nodded his head and turned back to face her. 'You'd better stay here, in this house,' he said, still in that odd, expressionless kind of voice. 'Just while you get yourself sorted out.'

'But what about you?'

He gritted a hard smile. 'What *about* me, Abby?'

'Wh-where will you stay?' Or was that a stupid question? There would probably be legions of women all queuing up to offer him the use of their beds.

'There are such things as hotels, you know.'

She stared at him, stricken by the repercussions of her words.

'But I didn't mean—'

'Oh, yes, you did,' he returned grimly. 'You meant

every word of it, so don't backtrack now. I suggest that you contact the employment agency which my friend Sandie runs—I'll leave her card for you on the bureau. Until you're earning, you can use one of my accounts...' He saw her expression and his mouth twisted. 'Oh, don't worry, Abby, you can pay me back every damned penny!'

'And, will I...?' She swallowed, suddenly aware of what she was in danger of losing.

He paused in the middle of buttoning up his shirt and looked up. 'Will you what?'

'Will I see you?'

'No.' He shook his dark head resolutely. 'My job here is almost over. Afterwards I intend flying to the States.'

She forced herself to be strong. Through her own stupidity she had already failed in one marriage. If she married Nick, then it had to be for all the right reasons.

If he still wanted her...

CHAPTER TEN

'I'M VERY SORRY,' said the beautiful blonde with the sexy New York accent, 'but Mr Harrington is in a meeting.'

Abigail put her slim leather clutch-bag down on the reception desk and gave the girl a winning smile. 'He'll see me,' she predicted confidently.

The blonde looked extremely doubtful. 'He never interrupts a meeting—'

'Look,' said Abby, her poise and her temper beginning to waver. 'My name is Abigail Howard. Why don't you just ring through and tell him I'm here, and let him decide for himself?'

The blonde shrugged, giving Abigail a look which said quite clearly that she did *not* welcome pushy Brits who came in and tried to tell her how to do her job! 'Suit yourself.'

Abigail pretended to study the magnificent black sculpture which stood in the centre of the air-conditioned marble foyer, still slightly bemused by her surroundings. When Nick had told her that the headquarters of his business were in the Big Apple, she hadn't realised that the size of the building itself could almost have rehoused the United Nations!

She unashamedly listened into the conversation the blonde was having.

'No, Mr Harrington,' she was saying. 'That's what I told her.' The pale blonde hair swung slightly as the receiver was transferred from one shell-like ear to the other. 'Her name is Abigail Howard.' She listened, and then smiled. 'Sure. I'll tell her.'

She replaced the receiver and turned to Abigail, who was already preparing to walk towards the door she was certain led into Nick's inner sanctum.

'Mr Harrington is very *sorry*—' the blonde emphasised the word insincerely '—but he really can*not* interrupt his meeting. However, he said if you'd like to wait he'll be happy to see you just as soon as he has a moment.'

Abigail felt like flouncing out with a few, well-chosen words to be given to *Mr* Harrington when he cared to put in an appearance, but she reminded herself that this would not be a very mature response to what was only, after all, what she might have done herself if the situation had been reversed.

She frowned. Or would she?

Could she really have carried on blithely conducting a meeting, however important, knowing that Nick was in the foyer waiting for her?

Somehow she doubted it. Particularly, she reminded herself, when they hadn't seen each other for almost a year.

'Would you like some coffee?' the blonde asked.

What she would like was a very large and very calming brandy, but she needed to be in command of all her senses when she saw Nick again. This meeting was much too critical to risk with a muddled head.

'No, thank you,' she heard her voice say, with surprising composure, and went to sit down on one of
the black leather sofas which lined the foyer, taking
a paperback out of her handbag and settling down
with the intention of reading it while she waited.

The seconds ticked slowly by. Abigail was reminded of a book she had once read, written by a
man in prison. How each minute had seemed like an
hour, each hour like a day.

The print of the book she had in front of her—a
book she had previously been reading with a huge
amount of enthusiasm—now danced before her eyes.
She was aware of the blonde stealing the occasional
glance at her, with triumph etched all over her perfect,
uniform features, no doubt, thought Abigail grimly.

How *dared* he?

How dared he keep her waiting like some little min-
ion, publicly humiliated in front of his receptionist?

She put her book back in her bag and stood up.

The receptionist looked up with a glint of barely
contained crowing in her eyes as Abigail marched de-
terminedly towards the desk.

'Could you please tell *Mr* Harrington—' Abigail
drew in a deep breath '—that I have better things to
do all day than dance attendance on him. If he wishes
to see me, I'm staying at the Plaza. But he may have
to wait,' she added, as, with a tight smile and her head
proudly held up high, she marched towards the re-
volving doors.

Back in her suite, she ordered a pot of coffee and
then stomped up and down the room, still fuming,

oblivious to the panoramic city-view from her hotel window. In front of the wardrobe sat her unpacked suitcase.

She had flown into Kennedy Airport, checked into the hotel, and gone straight over to Nick's head-quarters without even pausing to renew her lipstick. Well, more fool her!

She sat down on the edge of the bed and scowled.

He hadn't even had the courtesy to stop what he was doing and say hello, and that was after nearly a whole year of not seeing her! A year in which their only communication had been when she had faxed him six months ago, to say that she would no longer be using the account he had left open for her. And the brute hadn't even bothered to fax her back!

There was a tap on the door and Abigail leapt to her feet to answer it, but it was only room service with her tray of coffee and she had to force herself to sound enthusiastic as she took it.

She drank two cups of coffee, feeling as gloomy as she had ever felt in her life, thinking that her bid for independence had come to this, when there was an-other knock on the door. Only it was louder this time, and much more authoritative, and she replaced her empty coffee-cup on the saucer with a shaking hand, telling herself that it was probably only room service again.

It wasn't.

It was Nick. In the living, breathing flesh. And Abigail actually felt her knees weaken as she feasted her eyes on the real thing after a year of having to make do with an old photograph.

He was wearing an amazing-looking suit, superbly cut in the finest navy wool. His shirt was so white it almost dazzled her, and he had knotted his emerald silk tie with his customary carelessness, which had her itching to straighten it.

His hair was slightly longer than she remembered it, and the expression on his face looked nothing more than mildly curious, a light glinting at the back of the green eyes which made her long to hurl herself into his arms.

But she didn't dare.

'Hi,' he said lazily, in that tingle-inducing velvet voice. 'Aren't you going to invite me in?'

She remembered the cursory way he had dealt with her back at his office and turned on her heel to stalk back into the room without answering, heaving a secret sigh of relief, nonetheless, when she heard him quietly shut the door behind him.

She turned to face him. 'Yes, I'll invite you in!' she declared. 'It's only courteous, after all. I wouldn't leave *you* hanging around like a summer cold—not after a year!'

The merest quirk of amusement tugged at one corner of the delectable mouth. 'Oh? You've been ticking the months off, have you, Abby?'

'As a prisoner would, you mean?' she returned coolly, and he laughed.

He held his palms out in an easy, expansive movement. 'It was an important meeting,' he purred. 'And you wouldn't want me jeopardising future business for a meeting which could so easily be postponed, now, would you, Abby? Especially as I hear such glowing reports from London about your business acumen.'

Abby chose to ignore the compliment. So she had been relegated to the slot of an easily postponed meeting! She bristled with fury. 'Don't give me that, Nick! You're powerful enough and in demand enough to lay down whatever terms you want. And if you haven't got the decency to greet an old friend—'

She was moving to storm off—she was not quite sure where to—when he reached out and caught her by the wrist, gently levering her towards him so that she was close enough to feel the warmth which radiated from his body.

'Let's start all over again, shall we?' he suggested lazily, and kissed her.

She felt that her pride ought to show a little resistance, and she struggled for all of ten seconds before allowing herself to succumb body and soul to that kiss. She wasn't sure just how long it went on for; all she knew was that, when they finally came up for air, she was utterly, utterly shaken by it, and so, judging from the rather dazed expression on his face, was he.

'Wow!' he murmured softly. 'Let's do that again—'

But Abigail pulled herself away from him, even though it tore her apart to do so. 'Nick, I need to talk to you.'

He gave a sigh, and loosened his tie before pulling

it off his neck completely. He threw it over the back of a squashy, apricot-coloured sofa and then sat down, stretching his long legs in front of him. 'I had a feeling you might say that,' he said ruefully. 'Come and sit down and talk, then, Abby.'

'Only if you promise not to—'

'Lay another finger on you?' he mocked. 'Sorry, sweetheart—that's the kind of condition I won't agree to.'

The darkly intent look in his eyes thrilled her to the bone, and she went over to the sofa and, very deliberately and self-consciously, sat as far away from him as was possible without falling off, then turned to look at him, wondering how best to say what she had to say.

'Do you still want to marry me?' she blurted out, and, when he shook his dark head, her heart plummeted alarmingly into her boots.

'You d-don't?'

'I think that question should be the last thing we talk about, not the first,' he told her gently. 'Don't you?'

His reply shook her confidence more than she cared to admit to herself, but this was a risk she had known she would be taking. A risk she had acknowledged at the time. She could not now bury her head in the sand and wish that she had marched him up the aisle at the first time of asking.

'Did you make the right decision?' he persisted.

She nodded her head slowly. 'Yes. But it certainly wasn't the easiest choice.'

'But the easiest isn't always the best,' he offered softly.

'I missed you,' she said suddenly, unable to hold it back any longer.

'And?'

'I love you and I want to spend the rest of my life with you.'

'And?'

'Are you trying to make this difficult for me?' she asked him suspiciously.

'As a kind of reparation for having turned me down?' he mused. 'It's an interesting idea, but—no. And why should it be difficult for you to tell me your true feelings, Abby?'

'You haven't told me yours. You never told me you loved me!'

'You didn't give me a chance,' he pointed out. 'And if I had persisted and managed to convince you of the depth of my feelings a year ago, then you probably would have accused me of emotional blackmail. And perhaps you would have been right,' he reflected thoughtfully.

Her heavy-lidded blue eyes looked very large in her face. 'What do you mean?'

'Just that it was all too much, too soon. And not just too soon to leap into a brand-new relationship. You needed to grieve over Orlando, didn't you?'

She nodded her head slowly. 'I guess I did, in a way. I needed to let go of all the bad feelings I had for him, and to remember the good bits. And there were good bits,' she defended, rather anxiously.

'Of course there were,' he agreed gently. 'And you mustn't ever try to deny them—not to me, or to yourself. You aren't a fool, and you would never have married him if your feelings for him hadn't been strong.'

'I went to visit his parents,' she told him, her face sobering with the memory. 'In Spain. That's where they live.'

'And did that help?'

'It helped them,' she replied, in a soft, sad voice, remembering the stricken faces and confusion of the elderly couple as they'd sought to make some sense of their son's short life. 'I gave them lots of photos of him.' She gave a rueful smile. 'There were plenty of those. Orlando *loved* having his photo taken!'

'Good.' He rubbed the back of his neck with his hands, and Abigail was suddenly aware that she wasn't the only one suffering from tension. His eyes were questioning. 'So now you've come to me?'

'I don't know if you still want me,' she said quietly.

He smiled. 'Oh, yes, you do, Abby,' he responded softly. 'You only have to look in my eyes to see that.'

Abigail could have lost herself in that intense green light, but Nick had still to find out the truth about her. And would he still want her then? she wondered, swallowing down the lump of fear which constricted her throat.

Did he read the trepidation in her eyes? she wondered. Was that why he took hold of her hand, lifted it to his lips and planted a kiss there of such sweet tenderness that it made her almost want to cry?

'I love you, Abby, sweetheart,' he told her softly. 'I want to be your friend, your partner and your lover.' His voice deepened with dark, delicious intent. '*Especially* your lover,' he murmured, and kissed her hand again. 'So will you marry me, please? Soon?'

She leapt up off the sofa like a frightened horse and began to twist the silver ring she wore on her little finger. 'Why talk of weddings?' she babbled. 'Who needs to get married these days? Let's just go to bed!' she blurted out.

He was watching her very closely. 'Abby,' he said softly, his eyes never leaving her face.

'Wh-what?' She felt like a cornered fox.

'Are you going to tell me about it?'

He had risen from the sofa and was moving towards her, and suddenly he was next to her, pulling her into his arms.

She wanted to bury her face into his chest in order to hide it, but he wouldn't let her, lifting her chin up with a firm but gentle forefinger.

'Now tell me,' he commanded.

She nodded. Perhaps it was better this way—in the cold light of day, so to speak. He could always leave. Whereas if she left telling him until they were in bed...

'I'm a virgin!'

He nodded his head slowly. 'Go on.'

She looked at him suspiciously. This had not been what she had anticipated at all. She had visualised shock or, at worst, a kind of mocking scorn—not this calm, untroubled acceptance. But the truth would shock him.

'You don't know what I'm saying!' she told him.

'I know,' he responded. 'More than you imagine.'

'You can't!'

'Try me?' he suggested.

'I'm not a virgin out of choice,' she whispered. 'I'm a virgin because we couldn't make love. It was *my* fault! Orlando had had lots of lovers before me. And afterwards...' Her voice trembled. 'He told me I wasn't a normal woman. He said—'

But Nick was never destined to hear Orlando's thoughts on the subject, because he bent his head and kissed her, with that same tender, aching sweetness as before.

'Nick...' she began nervously, but he shook his head quite firmly, took her over to the bed and sat them both down on the edge of it, before looking seriously into her eyes.

'Abby, darling, I love you. Understand? And that's the bottom line. Nothing else matters. Making love isn't the be-all and end-all of our relationship.' He felt her shiver with nerves. 'But the longer we wait, the more you're going to worry about it, and the bigger the problem it's going to become. And it isn't going to be a problem, sweetheart. Honestly. Not for us. And now...' He smiled into her big blue eyes as he looked down into her face, a smile that was laced with anticipation and tenderness.

'Now?' she echoed nervously.

'Now you're just going to have to trust me.'

Nick collapsed back onto the heap of pillows and looked disbelievingly at the ceiling.

'Wow!' he murmured softly.

Snuggling into the pillow, Abby smiled.

Eventually he leaned over to click on the bedside lamp, then turned to prop himself up on his elbow to watch her. 'Wow!' he said again.

Abby cuddled up to him, yawning hugely. 'Does it always make you feel this marvellous?' she murmured. 'Like you want to run out in the street and whoop for joy?'

'Not always,' he told her, with a smile which told her quite clearly that she didn't look capable of running *anywhere* at that moment! 'In fact, it's never made me feel quite like this before.'

'How?'

'Just that, with you, I have the feeling that this is how making love was intended to be.'

'And that is?'

'Just perfect,' he whispered, and she stared into his eyes happily, not doubting him even for an instant.

'There was an almost spiritual quality to it,' he mused, shaking his dark head as though he still couldn't quite believe it, 'which has always been lacking before. And which I never really believed in. But maybe that's because I've never been in love before.'

Love! Abigail felt even *more* tingly—if that was possible—with every last inhibition about the past gradually seeping out of her. 'Did you guess before I told you?' she asked him, laying her head on his warm, broad chest and listening to the slowing down of his heart. 'That I was still a virgin?'

'I guessed that something was wrong,' he answered slowly. 'Because you tensed up so much during foreplay. Except for that one memorable time in Kensington—'

'Nick, don't…' she said, blushing.

He smiled. 'Why not? I *like* remembering it. I happen to *like* watching you have an orgasm. I intend to do a lot of that during our married life.'

'Oh, darling,' she cooed into his ear happily.

'Anyway,' he continued sternly, 'non-consummation of marriage isn't exactly uncommon, you know. Particularly not in your case, where Orlando had cold-bloodedly married you to get his hands on your fortune. Your mind was doing you a favour, really. Protecting you by making your body unable to accept him. It may be selfish of me, but I—for one—am delighted that he didn't know you in the way I have just known you—naked and loving and compliant and utterly and delightfully passionate.'

He twisted a strand of honey-coloured hair around one long finger. 'I knew all that was bubbling away underneath the surface, just waiting to be unleashed. But I also knew that it had to come when *you* were ready for it to. No pressure from me—in fact, you needed a break from any kind of pressure. And that's why I did my best to keep you at arm's length.' He gave her a rueful smile. 'Until I could resist you no longer.' He kissed the tip of her nose. 'But you shouldn't feel a freak about the past, sweetheart.'

'Orlando tried to make me feel a freak,' Abby admitted painfully. 'He taunted me with it regularly—'

'Which must have only exacerbated the problem?' he hazarded.

'Yes,' she admitted unhappily. 'And then he threatened to publicise the fact.'

'That's why you allowed him free access to your fortune?' he guessed.

She nodded. 'Yes.'

He swore very softly beneath his breath. 'I should have gone with my gut instinct that he was wrong for you,' he said to himself, almost bitterly. 'But part of me was appalled that my main reason for wanting to stop the marriage was because I wanted you for myself. Self-interest is no basis for trying to change someone's life irrevocably. And you did such a good job of convincing me that you were in love with him…'

'I told you, I was frightened. Insecure.' And too full of self-doubt ever to dream that Nick could have cared for her.

'I should have protected you. Looked after you.' He shook his head. 'Until I could manage to persuade you that *I* was the only man for you.'

'I think I would have needed very little persuasion.' She traced the outline of his mouth with a tremulous finger. 'But it would not have been the right thing to do, you know, Nick. I would have gone from one gilded cage to another. I would never have had the chance to develop and grow the way that I have done. I needed to be on my own. To support myself.'

'And how,' he breathed admiringly, before his eyes darkened with a look that made her begin to tremble with excitement. 'I have had regular reports from Sandie that you have the makings of a first-class businesswoman.'

'I *hope* that I've got the makings of a first-class mother, too,' she told him in earnest, loving the warm smile which lit up his green eyes.

'Oh, I don't think *that* was ever in question,' he murmured, his gaze drifting irresistibly to the pink-flushed skin above her creamy breasts. 'But, before I make love to you again, or rather,' he corrected, with a satisfied look which had Abigail hiding a secret smile, 'before *you* make love to *me*...'

'Yes, Nick?' she questioned serenely.

'I have a present for you.'

'Mmm?'

'Wait here.'

'I'm not going anywhere,' she told him content-edly, and watched him walk unselfconsciously across the room to retrieve the briefcase he had brought with him. A lot of men might have looked ridiculous wear-ing not a stitch of clothing and carrying a briefcase— but not Nick! Nick looked heavenly whatever he was wearing. Or not wearing, Abigail thought ecstatically.

He brought the briefcase over to the bed.

'What is it?' she asked him curiously.

'See for yourself,' he answered with a smile, and up-ended the case at her feet.

Multicoloured light dazzled and sparkled in a glittering stream as jewellery spilled out onto the bed. A fortune in diamonds, emeralds, sapphires and rubies all vied for her attention, and Abigail sat up immediately, her brow furrowed.

'My mother's jewellery?' she whispered. 'That Orlando sold?'

He nodded. 'The very same. For you.' He extracted a thick cream parchment envelope from the top of the gems and handed it to her. 'Also the deeds to the New York apartment,' he said, seeing her mystified expression. 'I wanted you to learn to stand on your own two feet, sweetheart,' he explained. 'But I also felt that you deserved what was rightfully yours.'

But Abigail didn't much care for jewels or property deeds any more; what she had was infinitely more precious—she had Nick.

She stood up and put her arms around him and rested her cheek against his bare shoulder. 'Oh, Nick,' she said softly. 'I do so love you.'

'Well, that's good.' He smiled. 'Because I'm yours—' he began to run his hands lovingly over her body '—to have and to hold.'

'Oh,' she observed thoughtfully, then let her fingers trickle slowly down his chest to alight upon and strokingly massage the most vulnerable part of him.

'Abby,' he groaned helplessly. 'Where on earth did you learn to do that?'

'I've read a lot of books in the year we've been apart,' she told him innocently, as she slid seductively to her knees in front of him.

She had decided that if anyone could unlock the door to her sexuality then Nick could—he was that kind of man—and she had read enough erotic literature in the intervening year to help her make the most of it! It was going to be a long and happy marriage....

'What—*sort* of books,' he gasped, as she began to work some kind of magic with her mouth.

'Why don't you come down here?' she purred. 'And I'll show you.'

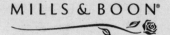

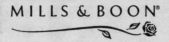

4 FREE

books and a surprise gift!

We would like to take this opportunity to thank you for reading this Mills & Boon® book by offering you the chance to take FOUR more specially selected titles from the Presents™ series absolutely FREE! We're also making this offer to introduce you to the benefits of the Reader Service™—

★ FREE home delivery
★ FREE gifts and competitions
★ FREE monthly newsletter
★ Books available before they're in the shops
★ Exclusive Reader Service discounts

Accepting these FREE books and gift places you under no obligation to buy, you may cancel at any time, even after receiving your free shipment. Simply complete your details below and return the entire page to the address below. *You don't even need a stamp!*

YES! Please send me 4 free Presents books and a surprise gift. I understand that unless you hear from me, I will receive 6 superb new titles every month for just £2.20 each, postage and packing free. I am under no obligation to purchase any books and may cancel my subscription at any time. The free books and gift will be mine to keep in any case.

P8XE

Ms/Mrs/Miss/Mr..............................Initials ....
BLOCK CAPITALS PLEASE

Surname ....

Address ....

....

....Postcode................................

Send this whole page to:
THE READER SERVICE, FREEPOST, CROYDON, CR9 3WZ
(Eire readers please send coupon to: P.O. BOX 4546, DUBLIN 24.)